S0-ARL-192

# A COMEDIAN DIES

## Simon Brett

A DELL BOOK

Published by
Dell Publishing Co., Inc.
1 Dag Hammarskjold Plaza
New York, New York 10017

Dell ® TM 681510, Dell Publishing Co., Inc.

ISBN: 0-440-11371-7

Reprinted by arrangement with Charles Scribner's Sons

Printed in the United States of America

June 1986

10 9 8 7 6 5 4 3 2 1

WFH

*To Alastair,*
*who's quite funny sometimes*

COMEDIANS: 'The second oldest profession, which, like the first, has been ruined by amateurs.'

*Ben Warriss*

# Chapter I

FEED: Did you have a nice holiday?
COMIC: Oh yes, what a week it was. Only rained
twice—once for three days, once for four.

*Sun 'n' Funtime* at the Winter Gardens, Hunstanton
was, according to the posters that faded on bus-shelter
walls and the brochures that were shuffled on to
boarding-house coffee tables, 'A Summer Tonic, Music
and Laughter for All the Family'.

The queue that Charles Paris and his wife Frances
joined that wet Tuesday afternoon in September looked
as though they could do with a tonic. In most cases an
oxygen mask would have been more appropriate. Their
average age was about seventy-nine and they had the
washed-out look of torn bunting clinging to the grille of
a drain. These were the dream-realisers, enjoying either
a seaside holiday or, in some cases, the life sentence of
retirement by the sea.

The Winter Gardens reflected their air of bewildered
decay. Maybe once the iron framework had boasted
brighter colours than the local council's chlorine blue
paint, which fought a losing battle against the encrusta-
tions of salt and the eruptions of rust. Maybe once the
white planks which filled in the lower parts of the
frame had not been pitted and scratched and aerosoled
with lewd invitations. Maybe once the windows had not
been mended with flapping strips of polythene and none

had rattled, puttyless, like old teeth in shrunken gums. But in 1977 the Winter Gardens was a building which had given up the will to live.

Perversely, Charles felt quite cheerful. The depressing nature of his surroundings seemed, by counterpoint, to enhance his sunny mood.

It was nice being with Frances. That was the main thing. They were together, in another attempt to mend their marriage, which had never been quite the same after Charles walked out sixteen years previously. Since that time there had been so many attempts to mend it that the marriage, like an old tea-service, was bumpy with rivets. Each attempt started well, in an atmosphere of mutual tolerance, but soon degenerated into the old cycle of bickering. After each failure Charles left again, depressed, convinced that an acting career was incompatible with a settled home-life. And each time he drifted into some inferior affair, which gave him even less than the flawed marriage.

But this time it seemed to be working. At least, after three days it was still working. Maybe it was just that they were older, with Charles turned fifty. Maybe it was being in unfamiliar surroundings, in the anonymity and slippery nylon sheets of the Waves' Crest guest house, Hunstanton. Whatever it was, Charles didn't want to analyse it or talk about it in case it went away.

They bought a programme and found their seats well in advance of the rest of the audience, who were delayed by wheelchairs, crutches and other obstacles such as their feet.

'Well, what delights have they to offer to our jaded intellects?' asked Charles as he opened the programme. 'Hmm. It's a packed variety show, I see. Bill Peaky in *Sun 'n' Funtime*. Since I haven't heard of the star above the title, I'm not very optimistic that I'll know any of the others.'

'I'm sure I've heard of Bill Peaky.' Frances wrinkled her brow. 'Seen him on television or something. Comedian with a guitar, isn't he?'

'No idea. As you know, I don't watch television much. Only when I'm on. Which means hardly ever.'

'There must be someone in the show you know, Charles. After all, you're in the same business.'

'Different ends of the same business, dear lady.' In his best Actor Laddie voice. 'I am an act*or* in the legitimate theatre; these are mere variety artistes. Oh, things haven't been the same since Equity merged with that Variety lot.'

'Comes to the same thing really. It's just different forms of showing off.'

'With that attitude to my art, it's hardly surprising that you weren't the ideal wife for me.' But it was said without malice, just teasing. How long was it since they had been sufficiently relaxed together to tease each other? 'Anyway, who else is on the bill? Good God, programmes these days get more and more advertisements and less and less about the show. Ah, here we are—just between "Ladies, for the very best in Modern Hairdressing, go to Dorita's" and "After the show why not enjoy the best Tandoori chicken on the East Coast". Now, who is there? Hmm. We start with These Foolish Things (whatever they may be), then Karamba and Judy, Vita Maureen (accompanied by Norman del Rosa), Mixed Bathing, Lennie Barber and—Good God, that couldn't be Lennie Barber of Barber and Pole, could it?'

'Of who?'

'Oh come on, Frances, even with your limited knowledge of show business, you must remember Barber and Pole. All those radio shows after the war. And then telly. *The Barber and Pole Show*. It was one of the first big variety shows on the box. In the fifties. You must remember.'

'Oh yes, I do. That's right, they had all those terrible catch-phrases.'

Charles dropped into a gormless Lancastrian accent. 'Bepardon?'

'Of course, your party trick.'

'Yes, my one and only show business impersonation. Wilkie Pole of Barber and Pole. I used to do it all the time.'

'You can say that again. Particularly when you were drunk.'

'It's all coming back. What was that other catch-phrase Pole had? Oh . . . um . . . Oh yes.' Again the accent. 'You're rushing me.'

'I remember that one too. God, it seems a long time ago.'

'It was.'

'Why did they break up, Charles?'

'Barber and Pole? Wilkie Pole died. Right at the peak of their popularity. Late fifties. Then I seem to remember they tried to launch Lennie Barber on his own, but it just didn't work.'

'What's he done since then?'

'Don't know. Kept reading about him in the papers in the early sixties. Bad publicity mostly. Divorce, arrests for drunkenness, that sort of thing—all the symptoms of a successful career suddenly gone wrong. Then nothing. I suppose he's been on the bottle ever since. And who knows . . . maybe touring the clubs all that time, going lower and lower down the league. What a way to end up though—if it is the same Lennie Barber—playing way down the bill to some jumped-up comic nobody's heard of.'

'But everybody will have heard of him soon.' Charles and Frances turned in surprise to the voice from the row behind. 'Sorry to have been rubber-necking, Charles. I couldn't believe it was you.'

'Good heavens—Walter Proud. How are you?' Charles reached out and the two men shook hands. 'You know Frances, don't you? My . . . er . . . my . . . er . . . my wife,' he concluded with some surprise.

'Of course I know Frances.' The man leant across and kissed her effusively, enveloping her in the fumes of a rather good lunch.

From Frances' expression she didn't share the recognition. Charles came to the rescue. 'Walter's a television director at the BBC. I worked with him on—'

'You're out of date, Charles. I left the Beeb last year. We . . . um . . . didn't see eye to eye. I've gone over to the other side, gone commercial.'

'What, you're part of the Brain Drain? On the staff at one of the . . .'

'No, no, freelance. I'm only on a three-month contract at the moment, as a producer, but, if the project I'm on goes well, it's bound to lead to other things.'

'Sounds good. You enjoying it?'

'Well, er . . . Do you know Paul Royce?' The producer indicated a dark young man who was studying the programme by his side.

'No, I don't. Hello, I'm Charles Paris.'

'Hi.'

'Paul's one of the brightest new writers I've come across for some time. Straight out of . . . where was it? Oxford?'

'Cambridge.'

'Yes, and already been nominated for a UEF award for his first series. Radio thing, of course. Did you ever hear *The Three-Legged Giraffe Show*?'

'*The Two-Legged Giraffe Show,*' Paul Royce corrected testily.

Charles said sorry, he didn't listen to the radio that much and, anyway, what the hell was Walter doing at a matinée of a summer show in Hunstanton?

'Ah, Charles, that brings me back to where I interrupted you. We've come down to see Bill Peaky. The project on which I'm working is a fifty minute special with him. Bound to go to a series, should be very big. Paul here's going to be doing some writing for the show.'

'Not if Mr Peaky thinks the same of the rest of my material as he did of the first batch I sent,' Paul Royce interjected sourly.

Proud was momentarily thrown. 'That remains to be seen, eh? But, Charles, have you really not heard of Bill Peaky?'

' 'Fraid not.'

'He came out of *New Faces*.'

'Eh?'

'The talent show that ATV do. He won the All-Winners. I tell you, he's a very hot property. Going to be very big. We're going to see him after the show, talk about our series.'

Music tinkled upwards from the pit. Most of the pensioners had been tucked into their seats. The show would be starting in a moment. Charles felt he should say something else and flicked through his mind for subjects. Oh yes, domestic life. 'Angela and the girls well, Walter?'

'Angela and I got divorced two years ago.'

'Oh, I'm sorry.'

'Best thing, probably. I still see the girls at weekends. Sometimes. Work and . . . er . . . things permitting.'

'Ah.'

'Glad to see you and Frances are still together anyway.'

'Yes. Oh . . . er, yes.' Frances' hand found Charles'. He could feel it trembling with a suppressed giggle.

The lights began to dim and the noise from the pit grew louder. Walter leant forward and hissed, 'See you in the interval for a drink, eh? And maybe after the show we could go out for a meal or something . . . ?' Charles remembered from their previous acquaintance that Walter suffered from the television man's terror of being alone, the need to surround himself with people, to buy company with interminable expense account drinks, to extend every convivial evening as long as possible.

He didn't take up the hint about a meal afterwards, but commented on the chances of an interval drink. 'Likely to be tea, isn't it? Bars won't be open for a matinée, will they?'

'Oh no, they won't.' Walter Proud leant back in his seat. 'No.' He sounded deeply disappointed and Charles identified the smell that he had been conscious of since his conversation with the producer began. Neat gin.

The curtain of the Winter Gardens, Hunstanton went up to reveal These Foolish Things. They turned out to be a dance group of four boys and four girls.

In fact, they were not just a dance group, but the latest in a long line of dance groups, all of which had been started by a choreographer called Chuck Sheba (known in the business as the Queen of Sheba). The first group he created was called The Young Things, who enjoyed reasonable success in television, cabaret and stage shows, until personnel changes and internal dissensions led to their disbanding and reforming as Some of Those Things and A Thing or Two. This process of binary fission continued so that these new amoeboid groups split again; Some of Those Things became The Thing-Songs and The Best Thing. These Foolish Things, the group in Hunstanton, were born from the break-up of The Best Thing. But they retained the three trademarks which distinguished all Chuck Sheba's groups—namely, they all bought their smiles from the same shop, they all mimed to taped singing, and they all did the same dance. This dance consisted of kicking a bit, pointing quite a bit, turning round a lot and gyrating the hips a great deal.

And that was the dance to which the crumbling audience in the Winter Gardens, Hunstanton was treated. On this particular occasion it was done to music called *Do the Shuffle*, but that didn't make any difference.

The overamplified sound died as the eight dancers froze into a human fan. The lights were doused and the audience, against the odds, proved they were still alive by lurching into asthmatic applause. They then clutched their prescriptions in anticipation of the wonders of Karamba and Judy.

Karamba should have been billed as—and in fact made quite a scene with the local Entertainments Officer because he wasn't billed as—Karamba, THE INTERNATIONAL ILLUSIONIST, and Judy. He appeared in a greening tailcoat and top hat and, with the help of Judy (an escaped traffic warden in darned fishnet tights), he 'amazed the audience until they could no longer trust the evidence of their own senses'. The audience seemed in greater danger of losing the evidence of their senses in sleep than anything else. The tricks which Karamba performed were all right in their way (for people who like seeing coins disappearing into glasses of water, billiard balls passing through sheets of cardboard and strings of bunting being produced from escaped traffic warden's ears), but they were accompanied by patter of such stultifying banality that sleep was the only refuge. Everything Karamba said was delivered in the same relentless monotone, regardless of meaning or audience reaction. If he was truly, as his publicity claimed, the INTERNATIONAL illusionist, it must have been by virtue of his ability to be dull in many languages. His finale, a long-drawn-out illusion which apparently involved the burning of a five-pound note reluctantly donated by a member of the audience, received the most diluted of applause.

Charles strained in the darkness to read what delights would follow, but his effort was unnecessary as the next act introduced itself.

The curtain rose on a lady in a long pale blue dress, cut high at the waist so as to push her bosom up into a mould like a soap dish. She was not over-endowed and her bosom was spread thin like a birthday cake run out of icing. The woman's face was the sort that went out with ration books, dating back to the days when wives were called Rita and Valerie, and everyone looked like Vera Lynn. Her modern flowing hair style seemed only to heighten the anachronism.

'Good afternoon, everybody,' she trilled, 'my name is Vita Maureen and I would like to sing for you a little

bundle of songs, some of your old favourites, some
right up to date, accompanied, of course, by—on the
piano—Norman del Rosa.'

A tubby gentleman in a red smoking jacket and an
auburn wig twenty years younger than his face looked
up from the keyboard to acknowledge his applause.
Since there was none, he returned busily to his piano.
He played flashy chords, loudly, without any music in
front of him.

Vita Maureen continued. 'And first, in holiday
mood, what could be more apt than that lovely number
*On a Wonderful Day Like Today* . . .'

As the wind which blew uninterrupted from the Urals
vented itself against the exterior of the Winter Gardens,
Charles could think of quite a few tunes more apt, but
Vita Maureen was not to be daunted, and burgeoned
into song.

It soon became apparent that she was one of those
rare creatures who have gone out of fashion in popular
music—a straight soprano. Not for her the transatlantic
vowels and broken rhythms of pop. She sang everything
like a teenager taking an Associated Board music exam.
Every note was right and the interpretation was un-
sullied by the elaborations of pace and understanding.
Everything she sang sounded the same. Her finale,
*Bring On the Clowns*, was indistinguishable from *My
Secret Love*, which preceded it. She was frozen like a
defunct insect in the amber of musical comedy.

The warm applause of her superannuated audience
suggested that they wanted to get back into the amber
too.

The act which followed the lovely Vita Maureen and
Norman del Rosa came from the opposite end of the
musical spectrum. First, there was a longish delay, filled
with thumps and muffled curses from on stage, and
then the curtain rose to reveal a pop group called Mixed
Bathing.

Mixed Bathing was obviously a group in search of an

image, which had tried to cover all its options by
dressing each member in a different style. The lead
guitarist/vocalist affected electric green satin trousers
and a silver lamé string vest. The rhythm guitarist wore
a striped blazer and white flannels. The keyboard player
had on a black leotard and top hat, while the drummer
wore a complete army combat kit.

Musically they suffered in the same way and again
had tried to deal with the problem by playing a very
wide pop repertoire, in the hope that some of it must
inevitably suit their styles. And to ensure that it should
all sound indistinguishable anyway, they played at very
high volume.

The array of electrical equipment on stage explained
the long delay before the group's appearance. They
were walled in by banks of speakers and amplifiers.
When they launched into their first number, *Under the
Moon of Love*, those painted panes of glass in the
Winter Gardens' dome hitherto undisturbed by the
wind, joined their fellows in a cacophony of rattling.
The waves of sound fluttered the old-age pensioners like
sweet wrappers in a windy playground. It was a relief to
most of the senses when Mixed Bathing reached their
final earth-shaking chord and the curtain fell.

It next rose to reveal Lennie Barber manhandling a
small cart on to the stage. He was having difficulty in
doing this, first because his hands were encumbered by
giant mittens and, second, because one of the cart's
wheels had been caught by some offstage obstruction.
He gave a sharp tug and it lurched on. A rattle of
laughter came from the geriatric audience, uncertain
whether or not this was part of the act.

It was a shock for Charles to see Lennie Barber. He
was unmistakably the one who had starred in *Short
Back and Sides* on the radio and *The Barber and Pole
Show* on television, but the familiar contours of his face
had shrunk with age. The cheeks, puffed out with af-
front in a thousand publicity photographs, now hung

slack, and deep furrows scored the old laugh lines round his mouth into a mask-like parody. But the greatest surprise was the hair. The old sleek outline of black, raked back from a parting, had now fluffed out into a aureole of springy white. It was only the lack of Brylcreem and the passage of time that had made the change, but perversely it gave the impression that the old Lennie Barber was dressed up, disguised as an old man for a comedy sketch.

His costume also seemed wrong. Gone was the trade mark of the white coat from Barber and Pole's famous *Barbershop Sketch*; in its place the comedian wore a short red jacket over red and white striped waistcoat and trousers. On his head was a small red bowler hat. He looked like an old print of a comedian from a vanished age.

The mittens added to the incongruity. They did not fit the style of the rest of his costume and their great size suggested that they hid some terrible swelling or deformity.

Barber's material was also strange. He started on a sentimental note with a little song about being The Simple Pieman. The chorus was quite catchy.

> Don't ask my why, man
> It's just that I'm an
> Ordin-ary Simple Pieman.

When he came out of the song, he changed gear abruptly. He was no longer recreating an old music hall act; he was modern, sharp, even sick. It was a great change from the old days. In the shows with Wilkie Pole he had been robust, optimistic, slightly self-important, always ready to put down his gormless partner. But now he had tried to break out of the old mould and find a style of his own. Charles regretted the change; he knew he shouldn't, but he would have liked a wallow in nostalgia.

However, the comedian's opening patter echoed

Charles' mood, so it was not without appeal.

'Hello, how you all doing out there? Comfy? Right. I tell you, those seats out there are unbelievably comfy. Old girl we had in earlier in the year found them so comfy she stayed in her seat for a fortnight.' A pause. 'Mind you, she was dead.'

Charles and Frances seemed to be the only members of the audience who laughed at that one. For the rest it was too near the truth.

'Matter of fact,' Barber continued, 'we get a lot of dead people coming to this show. Well, I *assume* that's why nobody laughs.

'Talking of death, did you hear about the Irishman who tried to commit suicide by jumping off the top of the Empire State Building? He missed the ground.'

The preoccupation with death was not going down well with the audience. The act was dying on its feet. Lennie Barber changed gear. 'Actually, the place I'm staying here in Hunstanton, the landlady's a real character. First day I arrived I said, are the sheets clean? She said, yes, I washed them only this morning. If you don't believe me, feel them—they're still damp.'

From then on he was into the familiar territory of *Your Favourite Seaside Landlady Jokes*. The audience, which, like all audiences, felt more comfortable with jokes they had heard before, began to respond. The restraint remained, but there were a good few wheezy chuckles.

Charles found it strange. At the start Lennie Barber had had something, a certain attack, in spite of the audience apathy. But he had gone into the seaside land-lady routine with resignation, performing on automatic pilot. Though the audience preferred this Identikit comedy, Charles, as a performer, could recognise that the comedian had opted out. His comic potential was being diluted to nothing. Just as age looked like a disguise on the real Lennie Barber, so did this undistinguished style of performing. In fact, to call it a style was a misnomer;

it was lack of style that made it so colourless. But through the drabness of the performance, Charles could still feel the power coming across the footlights.

Lennie Barber's modest ovation was followed by the return of These Foolish Things to do their dance again. This time they were miming to *When You Need Me*, though only an expert would have noticed. However, there was a more significant change. One of the unalterable precepts of the great Chuck Sheba was that all dance groups should comprise an equal number of boys and girls. And, whereas in the opening routine there had been four of each, there were now four boys and only three girls. The seven of them continued with their smiles screwed in as if nothing had happened, but one couldn't help noticing. Charles found it rather funny. Four men would stand in wait; three girls would cavort across the stage and launch themselves into their arms; three men would twirl round with their burdens; and the fourth would also twirl round, trying to look as if he had a girl in his arms too.

The absence of one of the girls was made the more obvious to Charles by the fact that the missing one was the prettiest. All of them had a kind of lacquered, manufactured beauty, but she had looked more authentically beautiful than the others. Long bouncy blonde hair, sweet childish face, trim figure. Charles had found his eyes constantly on her during the opening number and now she wasn't there, he felt cheated. Still, she didn't come back and, at the end of the dance, the group spread out in another depleted fan, the curtain fell to a rattle of applause and the lights came up for the interval.

Walter Proud was leading the four of them to the bar in the hopeless quest of an interval drink, when he stopped and greeted a stocky man with a small bald head. 'Dickie.'

'Oh hello, Walter.' The man called Dickie spoke

without enthusiasm. He didn't remove from his mouth the cigar at the end of which two inches of ash hung precariously.

Charles recognised Dickie Peck, one of the biggest agents in the business. They had met when Charles had been working with Peck's client, Christopher Milton, on the troubled pre-London tour of *Lumpkin!*, a musical loosely based on *She Stoops to Conquer*. Dickie Peck had either forgotten this previous meeting or chose not to recognise Charles.

He also seemed anxious to get away from Walter Proud, but the television producer was equally keen to keep him in conversation. 'What are you doing here, Dickie?'

'Came down to see Bill Peaky.'

'About . . . ?'

'About a project.' The delivery was calculated to stop further inquiry.

'Ah. I'm down here to see him too.'

'Really? If you'll excuse me . . .'

But Walter wasn't to be shaken off that easily. 'Great act, isn't he, Bill Peaky. Really going to be very big. I mean, it's original. All that business with the guitar. Nobody else doing that. Except Billy Connolly. But he's too blue for the family audience. I like to think that the reason for Peaky's success is that he's up to date, marrying the old music hall comedian bit with the world of pop music that the kids understand. You know, they really identify when they see someone come onstage with an electric guitar. And yet he doesn't alienate the older audience either.'

Dickie Peck was plainly uninterested in Walter Proud's theories of comedy. 'Sure. Well, I'm going round to—'

At that point he was interrupted by the arrival of a thickset young man in a sharp blue suit and a heavy gold identity bracelet, who spoke with the brash confidence of an East End street-trader. 'Hello. Mr Peck, isn't it?'

'Yes.'

'I'm Miffy Turtle, Bill Peaky's personal manager. Actually, I also represent the group, Mixed Bathing, and Lennie Barber as well, but—'

'Nice little package deal you've sorted out for yourself with this show,' observed Dickie Peck shrewdly.

Miffy Turtle accepted the compliment from a fellow agent with a tense little smile. 'I heard you were out front this afternoon, Mr Peck, and thought I should make myself known. Gather you'd like to meet the boy.'

'Yes.'

'Well, if you come round to the dressing room after the show, Billy'd be just delighted. I'm sure we'd be able to find a bottle of something.'

'By the way, my name's Walter Proud. We met. I'm the television producer who—'

Dickie Peck answered Miffy as if Walter had not spoken. 'I have to get back to town rather quickly. There's a charity première tonight. I'd better have a word with Peaky now.'

Miffy Turtle was taken aback. 'Well, oh well, yes, I'm sure that'd be all right. Come on round. I'll show you the way.'

The two agents set off towards the pass-door by the stage.

'Oh, I think I'd better come along and see him now too. Come along, Paul.' And Walter Proud, with his writer in tow, hurried along to join them, uninvited. 'Actually,' he continued when he caught up, 'I was just off to the Gents, but I know there's one backstage.'

'You'll find the lock doesn't work,' said Miffy Turtle in a tone of voice which implied that he didn't want the producer with them.

'Never mind, I'm not proud. Well, I am, actually,' quipped Walter, and he tagged along unabashed, drawing the scowling writer after him.

Charles looked at Frances. 'Seems we've lost our company. Let's go and join the geriatrics for weak tea and Nice biscuits.'

The second half of *Sun 'n' Funtime* opened with the Shannon Sisters, who delivered a muzak version of *Don't Give Up On Us, Baby*. They were genuine sisters, four of them, dressed in identical scarlet catsuits. They were similar to look at and all of them not quite attractive in a different way, as if somewhere there was a fifth sister, a missing matrix, who really was attractive and of whom all the others were inferior copies.

The audience loved them. If only their grandchildren were like that.

Next came Los Realitos, a troupe of jugglers and contortionists who were about as interesting as jugglers and contortionists usually are.

Now all that remained on the bill were Bill Peaky and yet another dose of These Foolish Things for the finale. Charles was hoping that Peaky would be worth seeing; otherwise the whole afternoon was going to be living proof that variety was dead.

He felt a prod from the row behind and smelt the gin-fumes as Walter Proud whispered in his ear. 'This boy is good, really good. One of the most original acts around. Going to be very big.'

The curtain rose on an empty stage. Empty, that is, of human life; the tons of Mixed Bathing's hardward remained in evidence. And an electric guitar on a stand in the middle.

Then Bill Peaky entered in a follow-spot. He had a cheeky face beneath a spray of ginger hair and was dressed in a beige three-piece suit and high-collared purple shirt. The audience immediately burst into applause. Charles, it seemed, was alone in his ignorance of the show business phenomenon that was Bill Peaky.

The comedian picked the guitar up nonchalantly as he approached the front microphone. He was very self-possessed, confident that he would get the laughs when he opened his mouth. He grinned and the audience tittered in anticipation. Then he leant forward to the microphone to deliver his first line. As he did so, he struck an open chord on the guitar and took hold of the microphone stand with his left hand.

There was a loud report and a flash from somewhere. Bill Peaky's body snapped rigid like a whip. For a second his face registered surprise. Then agonising pain as he was flicked back from the microphone by the force of the electrical charge. He crashed into the pile of amplifiers, twitched violently and crumpled down in a dead heap on the floor.

# Chapter II

FEED: I heard on the radio this morning that the
    police are looking for a man with one eye.
COMIC: Typical inefficiency.

At the inquest on the Friday there were no surprises as
to the cause of Peaky's death. He had had the full force
of the mains going through his body and the shock to
his system had stopped his heart.

How the accident had happened was rather more interesting to the technically-minded. An extension lead
from the plug-box at the side of the stage to Mixed
Bathing's amplifiers had been wired incorrectly. Being
cheap High Impedance equipment, it had joined not the
Neutral wire but the Live wire with the Earth in the
jack-plug fitted into Peaky's guitar. This potentially
dangerous set-up need not have been lethal, if Peaky
had not touched the microphone stand. The microphones were part of the theatre's PA system, also High
Impedance, but correctly plugged. When Peaky
touched his incorrectly wired guitar and the microphone
stand at the same time, he became an unwilling link in a
mains circuit.

The immediate question that this raised was: why
hadn't the accident happened before? How was it that
Mixed Bathing's string-vested guitarist/vocalist had
gone through a whole act treating the microphone as an
ice-lolly and caused no shocks except to the audience's
ear-drums?

The explanation was quickly forthcoming. After Mixed Bathing's set, when Lennie Barber pushed on his pie-cart, a wheel had caught in the lead and snatched the wires out of the plug. Rather than mending it in the middle of the show, the broken cable had been replaced, during These Foolish Things' second appearance, by another made-up extension lead which had been found in the theatre's electrical store. It was on this lead that the Live and Neutral wires had been incorrectly connected.

So the blame for the accident, if any, lay with the person who had originally made up this lethal cable. According to the evidence of the local Entertainments Officer, who managed the Winter Gardens, the lead had been lying around the electrical store for some time and had almost definitely been made up by the previous Theatre Electrician, who had retired three years previously and died within six months of retirement. He had not been well during his final months in the job and this was not the first example of faulty workmanship dating from that period. For the sake of the man's widow, the Entertainments Officer hoped that the results of her late husband's carelessness would not have to be published.

So that was it really, Charles thought to himself as he sat in the cramped Coroner's Court. An unfortunate accident, which no one could have foreseen. The Coroner was bound to bring in a verdict of death by misadventure, with recommendations that safety precautions in the theatre should be tightened up.

Charles had watched the inquest with interest. Since his involvement in the strange affair of Marius Steen, violent death had begun to exercise an almost unhealthy fascination on him. Frances disapproved of this new hobby with its inevitable by-product of detective investigation, but that didn't stop her from following the inquest proceedings with consuming interest. It was a welcome diversion. Once you had exhausted *Sun 'n'*

*Funtime* and the Amusement Arcade, there was not a lot to do during a wet September in Hunstanton.

The little Coroner's Court was full, with intrigued members of the *Sun 'n' Funtime* company and representatives of the nation's Press, for whom the death of a momentarily popular comedian carried a brief news value. Bill Peaky's widow was also present, an attractive blonde girl in a black suede coat.

Apart from the Entertainments Officer, evidence was given by the policeman who had first been called to the scene of the accident, by the Police Surgeon who had examined Peaky's body, by the resident Theatre Electrician and by Charles (known as Chox) Morton, who, as Road Manager for Mixed Bathing, was responsible for the group's equipment.

Morton was an emaciated individual in dirty blue jeans and a colourless pullover. His pale sunken face was curtained with long, straggly brown hair. He seemed to be in a state of high nervous tension, constantly interlocking and unwinding his fingers as he gave his evidence. No doubt he was in a blue funk in case he should be held responsible for the faulty equipment.

The only other person to be questioned was Miffy Turtle, Peaky's manager, who was asked whether his client was usually careless with his electrical equipment. Turtle revealed that Peaky was most punctilious about safety and made a habit of checking out his guitar during the interval with a device known as a Martindale Ringmain Tester. He could only assume that the arrival of the well-known agent Dickie Peck in his dressing-room had led Peaky to omit his usual interval routine.

As anticipated, the Coroner brought in a verdict of death by misadventure, with recommendations that safety precautions in the theatre should be tightened up.

As Charles and Frances were leaving the Coroner's Court they heard someone bustling to catch up with them through the crush. They turned to see the pianist,

Norman del Rosa, auburn wig gleaming over flushed
face. 'I'm so sorry,' he said, 'but it is Charles Paris,
isn't it?'

Charles admitted it was.

'Norman del Rosa. We worked together on a pantomime in Worthing, remember. *Cinderella.* You gave
your Baron Hardup.'

'Ah yes,' Charles agreed vaguely. He remembered the
pantomime but he couldn't remember any Norman del
Rosa being involved in it.

His face must have betrayed his ignorance. 'Oh, you
remember, Charles. You were with that little dancer,
Jacqui, who—'

'I don't think you've met my wife, Frances,' Charles
interposed hastily. Jacqui had been one of his early pec-
cadilloes (who, surprisingly had turned up again in the
Marius Steen case), and he did not particularly want
Frances reminded of her. 'I'm sorry, Norman, I really
can't recall—'

'Of course, the name. I was called Bobby Marquette
then.'

'Ah yes. It comes back. I'm so sorry. With the change
of name and . . .' He just stopped himself from saying
'that frightful wig'. 'And . . . er . . . things, I just didn't
make the connection.'

'Think nothing of it, dear boy. Delighted to see you.'

At that moment they were joined by the lovely Vita
Maureen, who (surprise, surprise) turned out to be Norman del Rosa's wife. After exchanges of pleasantries,
since the musical double act showed no signs of leaving,
Charles commented conversationally, 'Nasty business,
this.'

'Oh, my dear,' cooed Vita Maureen tragically, 'you
have no idea, but no idea. What it's been like being in
the company for the last few days. Hell, darling, isn't
the word.'

'Everyone pretty upset over Peaky's death, you
mean?'

'But devastated, darling.'

'He was popular in the company, was he?' Charles' curiosity to find out the background to the death could not be contained.

'Oh, everyone loves a star, don't they, darling?'

From his experience in the theatre, particularly from working with an egomaniac called Christopher Milton, Charles very much questioned the truth of this assertion. Norman del Rosa also seemed to have misgivings. 'Well, my love, I'm not sure that—'

But his wife did not let him get into the flow of his objection. 'It really is such a pleasure to meet you both,' she interrupted. 'Quite honestly, there are so few people of one's type in a place like this. You must come and have tea with us on Sunday. You will still be here, won't you?'

And before Charles and Frances had time to marshall their excuses, they were committed to tea at four o'clock on Sunday at the Devereux Hotel.

When they got back to the Waves' Crest guest-house, Charles found a message asking him to ring his agent.

This was almost unprecedented. Maurice Skellern was the laziest agent in the business. Charles only stayed with him because he had no hopes of dramatic changes in his acting career and because he was too soft to face the inevitable scene of severing their association. Besides, Maurice was quite amusing and a useful fund of theatrical gossip. He never got any of his clients jobs, but he did keep them up to date with who was sleeping with who and how. Charles rang up about once a fortnight for his dose of backstage dirt.

But for Maurice to ring him . . . that really was something. Charles could not completely bottle up a bubble of excitement as he dialled the familiar number on the Waves' Crest payphone.

As usual Maurice went through his masquerade of pretending that the phone was being answered, not by him, but by one of a horde of forelock-tugging underlings.

Charles, however, knew that the agency was a one-man operation. 'OK, Maurice, cut the pantomime. It's me, Charles. What gives?'

'Ah, Charles. Thank you for ringing back,' said Maurice grandly, as if it were an everyday occurence. 'I've got you a telly.'

'A telly?' Good God. Was it possible? Could rivers flow uphill? Had Maurice Skellern undergone a personality transplant and joined that small élite of agents who actually get work for their clients? 'What is it?'

'It's an *Alexander Harvey Show*,' Maurice dropped casually.

'An *Alexander Harvey Show*?' Charles couldn't control the great surge of excitement he felt at the words. At last he was going to be recognised, not just as an adequate support player, but as a personality in his own right. Alexander Harvey hosted the most successful chat-show in the country, which kept millions glued to their armchairs every Saturday night to watch the famous coruscate with wit in a spontaneous atmosphere of carefully rehearsed ad libs. And now the quicksilver repartee of Charles Paris was at last to be accorded its proper recognition. He was to be a guest on the *Alexander Harvey Show*. 'When is it, Maurice?'

'Three weeks Saturday.' Then the agent added maliciously, 'Why, have you got something else big on?'

'Ha ha. No, of course I haven't. Because my bloody agent never puts me up for anything, doesn't know any important casting directors and is so in touch with the world of theatre that he thought the recent opening of Sophocles' *Oedipus Rex* was a world première!'

'Now, Charles, that was a genuine mistake. And it's very hurtful when you dismiss my efforts in that cavalier manner. After all, I told you about the auditions for the modern dress *Look Back in Anger* in Colchester. And I've just got you this telly.'

Charles apologised. 'Yes, I'm being unfair. Sorry. How did the telly come about?'

'Had a call from one of the Alexander Harvey researchers yesterday. Apparently they're doing some big nostalgia programme. It's the fortieth anniversary of the valve or something and they're going to recreate some of the great radio and telly shows of the forties and fifties.'

'But I wasn't in any of the great radio and telly shows of the forties and fifties.'

'No, I know you weren't. Let me finish. One of the things they want to recreate is one of the old Barber and Pole routines. You remember them . . . Lennie Barber and Wilkie Pole. Well, apparently a guy who's advising on the show, producer called Walter Proud— don't know if you know him—well, he remembered that you used to do a very good impersonation of Wilkie Pole . . . Pole died incidentally . . . don't know if you knew. . . .'

Maurice continued his explanation and Charles felt a burning blush spread over his cheeks. To have thought that he was actually wanted for himself, not just as a convenient comedy feed. He tried to recall if he'd said anything to Maurice that might indicate the way his thoughts had been turning. He decided he was probably safe.

'I won't be expected to talk?' he asked with slight distaste, as if appearing on a chat-show was his idea of a personal hell.

'Oh, good Lord, no. They'll have Lennie Barber on for a bit of chat. All you have to do is play Pole in the little sketch at the end. Only one day's rehearsal and the money's good.'

They went into some detail over the money. Charles, always amazed by the size of television fees, thought they should ask for a bit more on principle. Maurice was of the opinion that, if any fuss were made, the casting director involved would say thank you very much and find someone else. Charles decided, on reflection, that Maurice was probably right.

They then talked a bit about Bill Peaky's death and
Charles asked if Maurice had any form on the
comedian.

'Not a lot. Only got big recently. I've heard he had a
bit of a reputation for the ladies. Put it about a bit, as
far as I can gather. But that's all. Think a lot was going
to happen for him, though. Big talent. You seen his
act?'

'Not enough of it to make any meaningful judgment.'

'He was a real live wire, I believe.'

'You can say that again.'

Tea in the Lounge of the Devereux Hotel had probably
not changed for forty years. Charles kept feeling that he
was back in rep, playing some antiquated thriller, in
which the hostess, wearing a grey blouse and long tweed
skirt, dispensed cold tea, while the chief suspect, a
bounder in a blazer and flannels, handed round plaster
fairy cakes to the juvenile lead and ingenue. He was
maybe being a bit flattering to himself and Frances by
casting them in the young rôles, but Vita Maureen and
Norman del Rosa fitted their parts perfectly, even down
to the costumes.

And yet it wasn't a thriller. There was no crime. True,
there had just been a violent death, but that had been
shown incontrovertibly to be an accident. Maybe
something else would happen. Maybe Norman del Rosa
would step behind the sofa, cast his eyes down and
freeze with an expression of horror at the sight of an old
dowager with a knife between her shoulder blades.
Maybe Vita Maureen would open the cupboard to get
out her Dundee cake and be transfixed by the sight of
the under-gardener's body swaying on a rope inside.

So deeply was he immersed in his fantasy, it was quite
a shock to find that the tea was hot and the fairy cakes
soft enough to receive his teeth.

'We always stay at the Devereux when we are in
Hunstanton,' Vita Maureen was saying. 'They know us
here and I think the manager and his wife (charming

couple, Bill and Geraldine, you must meet them) are more than a little stage-struck. I mean, most of their guests are . . . well, not to put too fine a point upon it, dull, and a lot of them tradespeople, so I think we are a breath of fresh air.'

'Yes.' Charles nodded jovially, feeling some sort of response was required.

Vita Maureen continued, telling of other hotels around the country where she and Norman had stayed. Charles' mind wandered. Frances was keeping up her social façade well, nodding and smiling encouragingly, as if what she was being told actually contained something of interest. He felt a twinge of irritation. Why did Frances suffer fools so gladly? He knew it was unreasonable to condemn her. He behaved just the same himself, but . . . but.

Gloomily he recognised the symptoms. Soon the honeymoon would be over again. He and Frances would niggle away at each other until there would be a major row over something minor. Then he would walk out again and the cycle would restart. It was depressing. He'd felt really relaxed with her for the first few days, but since Bill Peaky's death he was increasingly on edge.

Bill Peaky, Lennie Barber. Comedians. Strange that Lennie Barber should be coming into his life again so soon. Coincidence.

Vita Maureen's monologue continued. Well, in fact it wasn't quite a monologue. Every now and then she would refer to Norman for confirmation of a date or the title of a show. And each time he supplied it, she would hurry on, hardly allowing him to finish his sentence.

Charles felt desperately in need of a drink. Maybe he should have had a real skinful at lunchtime, so that he could doze, anaesthetised, through this ritual of gentility.

Maybe he did doze. Certainly it was with a shock that he realised they were discussing Peaky's death.

'It doesn't do to speak ill of the dead,' Vita Maureen was saying, with discreet malice, 'but I'm afraid certain

people in the company will not have been wholly sorry
to see him go.'

'Oh,' said Charles with the same intonation that had
greeted her other, less startling revelations.

'I'm not one to spread gossip, but let's just say there
was a certain young lady in the company with whom he
was having a . . . thing. Or had been. I gather they broke
it off. Somewhat acrimoniously.' She smiled apologet-
ically. 'The dressing room walls of the Winter Gardens
are disgustingly thin, aren't they, Norman?'

'Oh yes, my love.'

'Of course, a lot of that goes on in the theatre. It's
always a great relief to me that Norman and I work
together. It means one doesn't notice other tempta-
tions. So much more satisfactory, isn't it, Norman?'
She turned on her husband the sort of smile snakes
reserve for rabbits.

'Strange, Bill Peaky dying like that, though, isn't it?'
Charles mused. 'I mean, if he was usually so careful to
check his equipment every day, you'd think of all days
he'd do it when a cable had been replaced.'

'But he did do it,' said Norman del Rosa ingenuously.

Charles looked at him sharply. 'What, you mean he
did do it on the day he was killed?'

The pianist blushed. 'No, no, I didn't mean that. I
just meant that he always did. Every other day, except
that day. Maybe he didn't know the cable had been
replaced.'

'I remember there was a terrible accident when we
were doing a summer season at Torquay. . . .' Vita
Maureen swept the conversation on.

But Charles was not deceived by Norman del Rosa's
cover-up. The man had seemed to know something and
the way he avoided Charles' eye confirmed the impression. An instinct for the untoward stirred within
Charles. When he got Norman del Rosa alone, he was
going to ask what he really knew about Bill Peaky's
death.

The opportunity came surprisingly easily. Vita

Maureen, who treated the Devereux Hotel as if it were their home, insisted on showing Frances round. Charles refused the guided tour, which made it difficult for Norman to avoid being left alone with him in the Lounge.

There was a silence. The pianist moved uneasily around the room, as if he knew the question which was coming.

'What did you mean, Norman?'

'When?'

'About Bill Peaky testing the equipment.'

'He always tested it. His manager said so at the inquest.'

'I'm talking about the day he died. Did he test it that day?'

'Presumably not. How should I know?' The man looked desperately unhappy, as if he knew that his weak personality could not withstand even the mildest of interrogations.

'I think you do know.'

No, it didn't take long. He broke immediately. 'All right. He did test it.'

'With his ringmain tester?'

'Yes, he came down onstage at the beginning of the interval like he always did and tested out his gear.'

'And presumably it was all right?'

'I don't know.'

'If it wasn't, he would have said something about it. Unless he was trying to commit suicide.'

'I don't know.'

'Why didn't you say anything at the inquest?'

'Nobody asked me.'

Charles thought that pretty unlikely. The police were sure to have asked all of the company whether they had any information relevant to the accident. So what was Norman del Rosa hiding?

'Why were you onstage in the interval?' The question was asked very gently.

'I . . . um . . . I left some music on the piano.'

'There's nothing wrong with that. You could have

told the police that. But it's rather strange, because I saw the show and you played throughout your spot without music.'

Norman del Rosa looked even unhappier. And yet Charles sensed that he did want to tell, that it would be a relief to get it off his chest.

'Well, the fact is . . . I didn't want Vita to know I was onstage. The fact is, there's a place in the wings where there's a sort of crack in the wall. It's just by the dressing room where the dancers . . .' He halted in embarrassment.

'I see,' said Charles softly.

'The fact is, Vita had once caught me looking through this . . . crack and . . . You must promise you won't tell her.'

'Of course not,' he reassured.

Norman del Rosa looked relieved. The confession had made him feel easier. Charles felt a wave of pity for the little man in his ridiculous wig. A Peeping Tom. The fact that he was spying on dancers made it even more ironic, since most of them were totally without shame, used to anyone and everyone wandering through their dressing rooms while they were changing. Still, in a way he could understand. Somehow he couldn't imagine Norman having much of a sex-life with the fastidious Vita Maureen. A man who had been married to her for a few years could be excused worse deviations.

'I'm glad I've told you, actually, Charles. Weight off my mind. You won't tell anyone, will you?'

'Of course not. You know what this means?'

'Well, I suppose it means that whatever was wrong with the cable didn't go wrong until after Bill Peaky had tested it.'

That was a rather naïve way of putting it. But it was typical of Norman del Rosa's timorous nature not to follow the logic through to its unpalatable conclusion.

Cables don't just go wrong. The cable which killed Bill Peaky had been incorrectly wired. The Live terminal had been attached where the Neutral should have been and vice versa. If the mains tester had not revealed this fault in the interval after the new cable had been installed, then it was a reasonable supposition that at that moment the wiring was correct. So it was a reasonable supposition that the wires had been subsequently reversed by a person or persons unknown. Which made it a reasonable supposition that Bill Peaky had been murdered.

## Chapter III

COMIC: I say, I say, I say, what's the best way to
   serve turkey?
FEED: I don't know. What is the best way to serve
   turkey?
COMIC: Join the Turkish army.

Polly, the solicitor's husky-voiced secretary, connected
Charles with Gerald Venables. 'Hello,' the actor said
buoyantly. 'I think I've got another one.'

'Another what?' asked Gerald cautiously. In the office he was all solicitor, very formal.

'Another murder.'

'Really? OK, spill the beans.' The interest was in-
stantaneous, signalled, as ever, by Gerald's descent into
American slang.

'Oh, I thought you'd gone off murder.'

'No, it's still more fun than contract-fiddling.'

'I mean, you didn't give me much help when
Charlotte Mecken was murdered.'

'No, but dammit, her husband was a friend of mine.'

'True. Have you seen Hugo Mecken recently?'

'Couple of weeks ago. Met in a restaurant.'

'What's he doing these days?'

'Drinking himself to death, so far as I could tell.'

'Yes, I was afraid that's what would happen.' Charles
paused, swamped by a wave of depression. What was
the point in his dabbling in detection when his efforts

brought so little happiness to the people involved?

But Gerald wouldn't let him brood. 'Come on, come on. What is it this time? Spear-carrier impaled on his spear? Stripper garotted with her G-string?'

'No. Did you read about Bill Peaky?'

'That comedian who got electrocuted out at Great Yarmouth?'

'Hunstanton, yes. I was there with Frances.'

'Ah, you two back together again. That's good.'

'Were back together. I'm afraid we've had another row.'

'Oh God—'

'ANYWAY . . .' Charles changed the subject forcibly. 'About Peaky . . .'

'What, you think his death may not have been all it seemed?'

'It's possible.'

'But surely the inquest . . .'

'The inquest may have been working on incomplete evidence.' Briefly Charles outlined Norman del Rosa's revelation.

'I see. Yes, it certainly does sound possible. Anything I can do?'

'I'm sure there will be in time. For the moment I just wondered if you had any background on Peaky.'

'No, nothing, except what one reads in *TV Times* or a newspaper. He was one of these showbiz mushrooms who spring up overnight. One day nobody's heard of them, then they do a television and—bang—everyone's talking about them. But I don't know anything about Peaky personally. Not really my end of the business, I'm afraid.'

'Nor mine. Though it may be soon.'

'What do you mean?'

Charles told Gerald about his booking on *The Alexander Harvey Show*.

'Oh, I remember. Wilkie Pole. That terrible character you used always to be doing at parties after we came down from Oxford.'

'Yes.' Into the accent. 'Bepardon?'

'God, that takes me back. Look, Charles, get me a ticket for the show. I'd like to be in the audience.'

'What, to see me do my act?'

'No, to see Alexander Harvey. He's a client. I did his divorce.'

'Divorce? I didn't think women were his thing.'

'He's not the first to have made a mistake. I think he still kicks with both feet, anyway.'

'Interesting.'

'Is there any rehearsal for the show?'

'Just the day before the recording. But Walter Proud's taking me out to lunch today to meet Lennie Barber.'

'I thought Walter was with the BBC. *The Alexander Harvey Show*'s the other side, isn't it?'

'Yes, Walter's freelance now. Sort of throwing ideas around to all the companies.'

'I see. Thought he was rather well placed at the BBC.'

'Yes, but he left. I don't know, reading between the lines, I think there may have been some sort of row.'

'Hmm. Anyway, you'll get a better lunch on ITV expenses. Where's he taking you?'

'Restaurant called Great Expectations.'

'I hope they're realised. Let me know when you get anywhere on the murder.'


Great Expectations had recently opened in that Notting Hill area which is so convenient for lunching from BBC Television Centre. It was a concept restaurant, themed wittily around the works of Dickens. A bust of the author greeted patrons outside the door and inside the walls were covered with prints from his novels. The motif was carried through to the table-mats and napkins; menu and wine list were held in leather folders like first editions. The waiters and waitresses looked as though they had escaped from the chorus of *Oliver*!

This High Camp had also invaded the food. Instead of being called sensible things like Tomato Soup or

Steak and Kidney Pie, the dishes rejoiced in such titles
as Sairey Gamp's Strengthening Broth or Mr Pickwick's
Noble Pudding. Beneath these fanciful names on the
menu, just to make the whole exercise completely point-
less, appeared translations of what the items really were.

Charles arrived a little late to find Walter Proud and
Lennie Barber already perusing their first editions. The
producer introduced them perfunctorily, but the comedian seemed engrossed in choosing what he was going to
eat. 'Have a lot of trouble with the old guts,' he confided to the world at large, as he sipped a large whisky.
' 'Ey, Walter, do you reckon this Martin Chuzzlewit
would have garlic in it?'

'I wouldn't think so. It says underneath it's toad in
the hole and I think all the food here is supposed to be
traditional English.'

'Well, maybe I should try that.' Lennie Barber didn't
seem convinced.

'How about a Tale of Two Cities?' offered Walter
helpfully. 'That's just two poached eggs on spinach.'

'Hmm. I'm never sure whether eggs help or hinder.'

'It's very plain. Sort of Oeufs Florentine.'

'That sounds foreign.' So Lennie Barber didn't want
any of it.

Eventually, he went back to the Martin Chuzzlewit,
which the tassel-capped waiter assured him was wholly
without foreign condiments, and a Sidney Carton
(tomato soup) to start with. Walter plumped for Fanny
Squeers' Pâté, followed by a Dombey and Son with a
mixed green Little Dorrit. Charles was a bit more ad-
venturous and ordered Quilp Fritters and a rare
Nicholas Nickleby. Walter consulted the wine list and
ordered wine as if his life depended on it. Lennie Barber
said he would keep drinking Scotch and asked for
another.

Charles was interested in the comedian. He had that
feeling, that even hardened actors cannot quash, of
being in the presence of someone special, a celebrity. In
spite of the downward spiral of his career, Lennie Bar-

ber had been, in his prime, one of the greatest comics in the land. His catch-phrases had been on everyone's lips. Charles wanted to hear the man talk. He also wanted to hear the man talk about Hunstanton and Bill Peaky. Unwillingly, because he liked what he knew of the comedian, he had to admit that Barber was a prime suspect. Professional jealousy of a cocky upstart might have provided a motive for the crime. And Barber had been pulling the cart that broke the cable in the first place. Investigation would be necessary.

He looked covertly at the comedian. The spray of white hair over the lined features was still a shock, but at close quarters the face seemed to have more of the impudence of the old Barber.

Another surprise was the hands. The strange outsize mittens in Hunstanton were explained by heavy crêpe bandages. Interesting. Those too must be investigated. But, first, social conventions.

'It's a great pleasure to meet you. I've been a fan of yours for many years.' He hoped it didn't sound meaninglessly fulsome.

Barber seemed to take it straight. 'Surprising the number of people who say that—that they've always been fans. What happened to them when I needed fans, that's what I want to know. People forget pretty quickly.' He spoke without bitterness, just acknowledging facts.

'I don't think anyone who heard them or saw them will ever forget those Barber and Pole shows. The number of people I've heard saying they wished comedy programmes were like that nowadays.'

'I've been available. The trouble is, the public never want anyone to change. They liked me with Wilkie—and so they should, it was a good act—but they've never been able to accept that that was only one style I could do. I mean, I've been developing as a comic all my life. Still am developing. And yet all the public wants is me back with Wilkie. When he died, they didn't want to know about me on my own.'

'It must have been quite a shock for you when he did die.'

'I don't know. We'd known for some months he was on the way out. Mind you, it certainly would have been a shock if I'd known the effect it would have on my career.'

'I meant personally.'

'Personally? Wilkie and I weren't very close. Obviously we spent a lot of time together professionally, but we weren't bosom mates. Anyway I'd been thinking of splitting up with him for some time, so his death sort of decided that for me.'

'But why did you want to get out of the double act? It was enormously successful.'

'Oh, sure. But it was holding me back in my career. You see, Wilkie was a grand feed, but that's all he was. I was the funny one.'

The arrival of the first chapters of their meal gave Charles a moment in which to assess this claim. Though it sounded arrogant, there was a lot of truth in it. Lennie Barber had always been the funny one. It was his face that one remembered, ballooned out with indignation, twisted with deceit or crumpled with disappointment. Wilkie Pole had been a funny accent and a couple of catch-phrases, but otherwise just a straight man. The ease with which Charles could imitate him and (presumably) step into his place showed the lack of strong identity.

And yet Lennie Barber had needed him. His subsequent fall from popularity had shown that. Wilkie Pole had been nothing special in himself and yet he had been the irreplaceable catalyst in the chemistry of a unique double act.

Barber was having difficulty holding his soup spoon with his swaddled hands. Some of the red slopped on to his bandages. 'Shit. Looks like the stump's bleeding again.'

It gave Charles the perfect opportunity. 'What happened? Have you lost a finger or something?'

'No. Joking about the stump. I got burnt. Bloody electric kettle in my digs at Hunstanton. It was faulty.'

Charles' heartbeat quickened. Faulty wiring could certainly give a burn. But it would be possible to get that kind of shock while sabotaging an amplified extension lead as well as from a faulty kettle. 'When did it happen?' he asked casually.

'A Sunday. When was it? Two weeks ago last Sunday.'

In other words, before Peaky's death. Charles realised the stupidity of his recent conjecture. Barber had had the bandages on when he did his act in the first half of *Sun 'n' Funtime*. And since the fatal fiddling with the cable had been done in the interval, that couldn't be how the comedian got burnt.

With this realisation came another, comforting thought. If Lennie Barber's hands were still so painful that he couldn't manage a soup spoon, it was impossible that he could have dismantled a plug and changed its wires two weeks previously. So, unless the whole business with the burns was an act, Lennie Barber didn't kill Bill Peaky. And that could be confirmed in time by a look under the bandages.

The germ of a further thought was also born. Two comedians in the same show, both the victims of electrical accidents. Was there a connection?

This chain of ideas didn't come to Charles immediately, but evolved while he continued to question the comedian about his relationship with Wilkie Pole.

'How did the two of you get together?' He knew he sounded like a show business page reporter, but he wanted to get to know the comedian and few performers can resist talking about themselves. Walter Proud didn't contribute to the conversation, but sat back complacently as if he had just introduced Gilbert to Sullivan.

'Met on the halls. We were both touring round in the early thirties. Only in our teens. I was called Charley Wobble then—my act was a few impressions and a pat-

ter routine. Wilkie was with a vocal harmony group
called the Songthrushes. Usual thing happened—I
wanted to try out a new sketch, which was two-handed.
He hadn't done anything like that, but said he'd have a
go. Bilston Royal I think the theatre was. Anyway, it
went all right with the audience and so, a couple of years
later, when I'd got some more double-act routines, I
looked him up again and we got together. '37, it was.'

He had responded in the style that Charles' show
business reporter approach demanded. The story had
been told many times before, but he was prepared to tell
it again, so long as no one expected him to get too excited about it.

'And then you toured the halls as a double-act?'

'Yes, a good few years of that.'

'And were you a success right from the start?'

'Good God, no. We died the death. I tell you, you
name any theatre in this country and we've died there.
There's no such thing as overnight success in this
business. You're as good as your last show. Even when
you've got a good act, it can suddenly all go wrong. The
audience just stops laughing. No reason, no reason you
can tell, anyway. They just suddenly don't find it funny
any more and you're back where you started.'

'So you and Wilkie Pole just plugged away at it,
doing the same act time and again until the audience
began to appreciate it?'

'No, of course not. Blimey, where were you brought
up—the Royal Academy of bleedin' Dramatic Art? A
music hall act is not a play. You don't go on doing it the
same until the audience likes it. You change it all the
way *so* that the audience likes it. Wilkie and I changed
the act every night, added little bits I'd thought of, tried
new things out. That way we got to know what was
going to work. I mean, take something like our barbershop routine, you wouldn't recognise that from the
way we done it at first. By the time we got it good we'd
changed every line, we were only doing the stuff that
worked. Mind you, an audience could still surprise you

and give you nothing, but at least we knew we were in with a chance. That act took at least five years to get going and we were still developing it while we was doing the radios and telly shows.'

Lennie Barber paused and poked rather suspiciously at his Martin Chuzzlewit, which had just arrived. Walter Proud took the opportunity to assert his entrepreneurial position.

'Actually, I wanted to talk about the Barbershop Sketch. I think that's the one we should do for *The Alexander Harvey Show.*'

'I knew it bloody would be.' Morosely Lennie Barber speared one of the sausages in his Martin Chuzzlewit. 'I done more routines than most people have had hot shits and all they ever bloody want is the Barbershop Sketch.'

'Well, it is a classic.'

'Oh yeah.' He sounded resigned. 'I feel like bloody Elgar must've felt—wrote all this acres and acres of music and all anyone remembers is Land of Hope and bleedin' Glory. Whoever he met, I bet they all said, "Show us your *Land of Hope and Glory.* Go on." He must've got bloomin' cheesed off with it.'

It was an unexpected parallel for the comedian to draw. Lennie Barber was more cultured than he might appear. For Charles it offered a new insight to the man's character, which was beginning to exercise a strong fascination.

However, what Barber said did raise immediate worries for him as a performer. 'Lennie, if it took you all those years of doing the sketch, presumably twice nightly, to get it right, how on earth do you reckon I'm going to be able to learn it up in one day of rehearsal?'

'No problem. It's because we done all that work that it'll be easy. I know exactly how that sketch works. Wilkie was only the feed anyway; I had all the lines. No, so long as you can get the voice right—and I presume you can, otherwise Walter wouldn't have booked you—it'll be all right. I'll give you the timing. You just do exactly as I say and it'll work.'

'I don't look a lot like Wilkie Pole.'

'You will in the costume, don't worry. He had the special wig, so's I could cut the hair, then that big moustache and the pasty face. Under that lot anyone who'd got two eyes, a nose and a mouth would look like Wilkie Pole.'

While not wholly flattering to his self-esteem as an actor, this was at least a comfort for the job in question.

'But, Lennie, if it was so easy to get someone to look like Pole, why didn't you take on a new feed after he died? Any number of comics have done that. Jimmy James kept on changing his stooges, why couldn't you do that?'

'Bloody hell, Charles, haven't I told you?' Lennie Barber now sounded quite annoyed. Other people munching through the Complete Works of Dickens looked over to their table. 'I wanted to do something else. I had been trying to get out of the Barber and Pole thing for years.

'Look, I'm a comedian, that's my profession, and like anyone in any other profession, I want to get better at it. I've been on the boards for fifty-six years and I'm still improving my act. I started in 1921, six years old I was, did a comic song and a dance. *Harry, What Are You Doing With That Hammer?*—that was the number. On the same bill as my Dad.' His tone softened with pride. 'Did you ever see my Dad? Freddie Darvill he was called—Darvill's my real name. He was on the halls all his life. Billed as The Simple Pieman—did an act with a barrow of hot pies. Sang, danced—did a lovely clog dance—not that he come from the North, Londoner born and bred, like me. He could do it all, my Dad. Taught me the lot.'

'I'm afraid I don't think I ever saw him.'

'No, I suppose you wouldn't have done. Too young. He died 1936, backstage at the Derby Hippodrome. Perforated ulcer.' The memory abstracted him for a moment and the watery eyes fixed in space. Then he turned to Charles with a gleam of malice. 'Still, I'm sure you weren't traipsing round the halls at that age. Getting your dose of culture down the bleedin' Old Vic, I dare say.'

Charles smiled indulgently, hoping to disguise the fact that Lennie Barber was absolutely right.

'I still got all my Dad's old gear. All his props and that. Look after them very carefully. In fact, I used his old pie-cart in a summer season I just finished.'

'Hunstanton.'

'Right.'

'I saw it.'

'Oh, did you?' For the first time in the conversation the comedian looked embarrassed. 'Well, I can only apologise. Not my greatest performance. No, I wanted to work up a new act there, you know, using some of my Dad's routines with the pies, but the audiences up there . . . Jesus. Like I said, you got to give the audience what they want and that lot of old biddies just wanted jokes they knew so well they could join in the punch-lines. I'm afraid I give up on that lot.'

'But you're still going to work up the new act, are you?' Walter Proud asked with professional interest.

'Oh sure, I will do it.'

'Because I'm still convinced that with the right sort of act, the right breaks, a timely telly show, you could make a very big come-back. Nostalgia's very big in the entertainment business.'

'Thank you very much.' The words were loaded with irony. 'If I make a come-back, it won't just be because nostalgia's very big, whatever that means. It'll be because I'm a bloody good comic. I'm going to go on being a comic and if it turns out that I'm what the audience wants suddenly, then I'm sure I'll be a rich and popular comic again. If that doesn't happen, it won't stop me working.'

'But don't you get depressed when it's going badly?' asked Charles, prepared to identify with the reply.

'Of course you do, but it doesn't stop you doing it. It's my profession. Look, an estate agent doesn't stop

estate agenting when a house sale falls through and I
don't stop being a comic when I get the bird. I get
depressed, sure, but it just makes me determined to do it
better. I'm not like that poor boy who used to do *I Do
Like To Be Beside the Seaside*, what was his name?
Mark Sheridan, that's right. He shot himself in Glasgow
when the audience hadn't liked his act. Well, that's not
my style. I just keep doing it.'

'But surely you want to get back to the success you
had in the forties and fifties?'

'Oh sure I'd like to get back. I'm human. That was
good, that was a peak. The money, for a start, being
recognised in the street, flash restaurants, showbiz golf,
Royal Variety Show, all that ballyhoo. But if it doesn't
happen, I'll still be a comic, that's all I'm saying.'

'I think it could happen again,' said Walter Proud
wisely, as if he was withholding some information on
the subject. Charles knew from his experience of
Walter's character that he wasn't.

'I don't think about it no more.' Barber took a swig
from his whisky glass. 'I've heard too many agents and
producers saying, this is going to be the big one, this
time it'll really take off. I tell you, I been discovered so
often, that I'm only glad all the discoverers didn't plant
flags on me. OK, a comic has peaks and troughs. I've
had my peaks, I'm lucky—a lot of comics never even
have that. My Dad never made it big. Always a great
comic, but nobody remembers the name. And what's
more, it didn't stop him working.'

The long exposition of his life seemed to have relaxed
him. He joked over the choice of sweets before plump-
ing for a Little Nell. 'I shouldn't really, but the old
guts don't seem to have taken the first course too
badly.'

Charles thought it might be a good time to find out a
little background to the death of Bill Peaky. 'Interesting, the Hunstanton show,' he began.

Lennie Barber quickly showed up the fatuity of that
as an opening gambit. 'Interesting? I would have

thought it was anything but bloody interesting. Now if you'd said boring or dull or terrible, I'd be right with you. But interesting—no. Summer season's always hell—even pantomime's better—but Hunstanton was the bottom. Nothing happened there.'

'Except the death of a comedian,' Charles offered gently.

'Like I said, comedians have died in every—'

'I didn't mean that. Bill Peaky.'

'Oh, him.' From his intonation, it sounded as if he had genuinely forgotten the incident. 'Was he a comedian?'

Walter Proud couldn't forget that he had actually been trying to set up a programme with the dead man. 'Oh yes, I think he was enormously talented. Would have developed into something really big.'

'Jesus, Walter, ever since I've known you, you've always wanted everything to be *big*. Back in Ally Pally days, when you were just a technical boffin with all the sound recording stuff, you were always talking about things being big. I don't know whether Bill Peaky was going to be big or not. Personally I couldn't see anything in his act. He had no technique, no experience. But I'm prepared to believe from the money they were paying him that somebody thought he had a future. But a short one, surely. The public will be fooled by novelty for a bit, but they soon get tired of it.'

'They didn't get much of a chance to get tired of Bill Peaky,' observed Charles.

'No. Mind you, the rest of the company did. A little of him went a very long way.'

'Not popular, you mean?' Charles overlaid his interest with casualness.

'You could say that. About as popular as a mosquito in a sleeping bag. Always going on about how great he was, how much money he was making, what a big star he was going to be. Fair got up everyone's hooter. No, he was riding for a fall. Just as well he snuffed it before someone helped him on the way.'

It shouldn't have been, but it was a shock to Charles to realise that most people still thought of the death as an accident. The presumption of murder had become so much a part of his thinking. 'Anyone in particular out to get him?' he asked with the same casualness.

'Like I say, no one liked him. Big-headed little runt. He was so rude to everyone. My God, the things he said to that poor little pianist, Norman del Rosa. But not just him. Everyone. We were all crap and he was God's gift to the entertainment business.'

'What about the girls? Did they like him?'

'If you mean was he shafting any of them, the answer was yes. I think he was trying to work his way through all the dancers.'

'These Foolish Things?'

'Yes. Maybe he thought when he'd had all of them, he could send off for a free badge or something.'

'How far had he got when he died?'

'He'd made it with a couple of them, I know. But I think he may have come unstuck with one called Janine.'

'What, she wasn't having any?'

'Oh no, not that. But she got a bit serious about him. He'd seen it as wham-bam-thank-you-ma'am, but I think she had something more permanent in mind. They had a fairly major bust-up about it. Lots of shouting in the dressing rooms and slamming doors.'

That confirmed what Vita Maureen had hinted at so decorously.

And suddenly something else slotted into place. Charles thought back to the show in the Winter Gardens, Hunstanton. To the end of the first half. When These Foolish Things had mimed and danced to *When You Need Me*. When, contrary to all the teaching of Chuck Sheba the great choreographer, there had been four boys and only three girls. Charles reckoned he could put money on the name of the missing girl.

In fact, to find the murderer of Bill Peaky, the first essential was to trace a Foolish Thing called Janine.

# Chapter IV

COMIC: An out-of-work actor came home one day and found his wife in a hysterical state, her clothes torn, her face and arms scratched to pieces. 'My God,' he cried. 'What happened?'
'It was terrible,' his wife replied. 'This man came round and raped me.'
'Who was it?' shouted the actor in fury. 'Who was it?'
'Your agent.'
'My agent? Did he leave a message?'

There was only one member of the *Sun 'n' Funtime* company over whom Charles had any hold. And fortunately Vita Maureen, anticipating a reciprocal genteel tea party, had given him their phone number in Dollis Hill.

Norman sounded guilty when he answered the phone, as if he had been caught in the lavatory with a dirty book. From what Charles knew of the pianist's character, it was quite possible that he *had* been caught in the lavatory with a dirty book.

'I'm sorry, Vita's out.' He didn't entertain the possibility of anyone wanting to speak to him rather than to his lovely wife. 'She's doing an audition for a new rock musical about the Boston Strangler.'

While Charles' mind strove to digest this incongruity, his voice said he didn't want to speak to Vita anyway.

'Oh.' Norman sounded desperately unhappy.

'It's about the dancers in the Hunstanton show.'

Of course Norman took it wrong. 'Look, you said you'd never mention that. Are you trying to blackmail me, because I daren't let Vita find out about—'

'No, no,' Charles soothed. 'I wouldn't dream of breaking your confidence.'

'Oh.' Norman sounded appeased but still suspicious. 'Then what do you want?'

'I'm trying to trace one of the dancers. Janine. She was the one who was having an affair with Peaky, wasn't she?'

'Everyone reckoned so. Mind you, I don't think she was the first in the company.' This was said with a kind of wistful relish. Maybe Norman del Rosa didn't confine his voyeurism to peeking at girls changing.

'And she had a row with Peaky on the day he died?'

'Yes.'

'When he broke off the affair.'

'That's what everyone reckoned.' Norman del Rosa was unwilling to answer anything off his own bat; he needed the support of majority opinion.

'And then she went off in the middle of the show?'

'Yes, she wasn't well. Gastric trouble.'

Fairly easy to fake. Lots of visits to the lavatory and nobody would question their authenticity. 'So, what . . . she went home?'

'Back to her digs, yes. Got a taxi. Actually . . . ,' Norman dropped his voice for the great daring of an opinion, 'I think it could have been caused by the emotional upset.'

Charles agreed, but didn't say so. 'Do you happen to remember when she got the taxi home? Straight after their opening number, or what?'

'She may have ordered it then. I don't think it arrived till the end of the interval.'

Giving her plenty of time to tamper with the amplifier extension. 'Look, I want to get in touch with this Janine. Any idea where she lives?'

Anyone would have asked why Charles wanted to contact the girl, but Norman del Rosa wasn't going to get involved. 'I don't know, Charles. I mean, I know where she was staying in Hunstanton, but she'll have gone from there.'

'Give me the address anyway. She must have told the landlady where she lived.'

Norman gave the information, again making no concession to curiosity. Maybe he regarded this as the price of Charles' silence over his own sad little secret.

'And if I don't get any joy there, do you know who the group's agent was?'

Again Norman obliged. Then, with ill-disguised relief, he put the phone down.

Janine's Hunstanton landlady had stepped straight out of *Your Favourite Seaside Landlady Jokes*. As she fulminated down the phone, Charles visualised a McGill postcard figure, arms folded righteously beneath her enormous bosom, bottom thrust backwards with rectitude, body swathed in a print overall and curlered hair scooped up into a red print handkerchief.

Basically she was offended by his call. And she let him know it. 'I keep a respectable private hotel and I don't give the addresses of my clients to any Tom, Dick and Harry who phones up out of the blue. I'll have you know, I only allow in a very respectable type of client. I don't want you to think that I'm prepared to act as a mere convenience. I don't set up assignations for girls who come and stay here. You ought to be ashamed at your age—chasing after young girls. She's not been here for weeks, anyway. I know you dirty old men, pestering girls young enough to be your daughters. Well, I don't keep a licensed brothel and—'

'Look, all I'm trying to do is to contact the girl to—'

'Don't you come the heavy breather with me, my man. Oh, I know your sort. You think just because a girl's a dancer, because she's prepared, for her art, to show a little leg on stage that—'

The pips went. Charles decided it wasn't worth putting in more money.

He stood irresolute by the payphone on the landing of the Hereford Road house where he lived. One thing the affronted landlady had told him was that he needed a cover. Unless he found some story to explain why he wanted to find the girl, all his enquiries were going to be met with the same suspicion. Maybe he even needed another identity to help him out. With a little bubble of school-boy excitement, he went into his bedsitter to look at his range of clothes.

The man who walked into the office of Alltalent Artistes in Berwick Street was wearing a trilby hat and a long beige mackintosh. The trilby dated from the days when men actually wore trilbies and the raincoat Charles had bought at a jumble sale during one of his economy drives and never worn because it was too big. He thought the image was not inappropriate to an insurance salesman. The potential shabbiness of the garb was offset, he felt, by a rather distinguished pair of silver-rimmed half-glasses and a slim black briefcase.

The girl in the hardboarded-off cupboard which served as reception was not impressed. She peered over her typewriter and the detritus of coffee-cups, publicity photographs and handouts that littered her desk. 'What do you want? If it's Danielle, French Model, that's up two more floors.'

'No, I wanted to come here,' said Charles in the precise tones of an insurance salesman, innocent of any activities of French Models other than modelling Parisian fashions. He had worked quite hard on the characterisation. He was using the voice he had developed for *The Fireraisers* in Newcastle ('Had I not known it to be a good play, this production would not have convinced me of its merit.' *Hexham Courant*). And if he ran out of motivation or vocabulary for his character, all he had to do was to focus his mind on his son-in-law, Miles Taylerson, who was a rising force in the insurance world and spent all of Charles' rare visits to his home trying to get his signature on to a policy.

Charles produced his carefully prepared identification routine. 'I'm from the Eagle Crown Insurance Company.' He didn't give a name; there was always the danger he might forget it. 'I'm trying to contact Miss Janine Bentley, whom I believe is a client of Alltalent Artistes.' Maybe the 'whom' was a bit much. Still, the girl was not a discriminating audience.

'Well, she doesn't live here. Why don't you try her home?'

'I have tried, but had no success at the address where we previously had dealings.'

'Hmm.' The girl still looked at him askance. 'I'll go and tell Mr Green you're here.'

She edged round her desk and through a door in the hardboard partition. Opposite Charles hung a publicity poster for These Foolish Things. As when he had seen them on stage, he was struck that Janine Bentley was the prettiest one. She intrigued him. There was a quality of innocence in her face that seemed out of place in a murder investigation,

The thinness of the hardboard which separated off Mr Green's office meant that Charles could hear exactly how the agent's secretary described him.

'There's a funny sort of bloke outside trying to contact Janine.'

'Oh yeah. Who is he?'

'Says he's from some insurance company.'

'Legit?'

'Dunno. Looks a bit weird.'

Weird? It is the actor's lot to have his performances dissected by ill-informed critics.

'You better show him in.'

The secretary came back into view and scuttled behind her desk as if Charles had rabies. 'Mr. Green will see you. If you'd like to go in.'

Mr. Green was a thick-set man, whose nose appeared to have been the victim of cosmetic surgery. The disparity between it and the rest of his heavy features made it almost impossible to conduct a conversation with him without staring transfixedly at the little button in the middle of his face.

Out came the identification routine again. Green looked at him in silence for a moment, assessing. 'I gather you're trying to contact Janine Bentley.'

'That is correct, yes.'

'Why?'

Still on prepared ground. 'A couple of years ago I sold Miss Bentley a life-insurance policy. Linked in fact to our property fund, which, I must say is doing very well at the moment with the current upturn in property values. Well, there has recently been a slight change in our company's manner of dealing with our client's investments and I wanted to discuss the new options available with Miss Bentley.' Pretty damned good, Charles thought to himself.

Green still looked at him. 'Janine never struck me as the sort of girl to go in for life-insurance.'

'Oh really? We are talking about the same Janine, aren't we? The one who dances with These Foolish Things. She obviously behaves very differently with different people. I mean, she went into the whole business of insurance with me in great detail. Very mature, responsible young lady. You wouldn't think it when you see her on stage, all flashing thighs and carefree bounce. But I find a lot of my clients are like that. Whatever they're like on the outside, sensible people do think about life-insurance . . . I don't suppose you yourself might be interested in any of the schemes that our company offers . . .' he added diffidently.

That was naughty. He shouldn't have got carried away. But fortunately Green reacted just as Charles always did when Miles got on to his favourite subject.

'I wouldn't under normal circumstances give anyone the address of one of my clients. You know, there are a lot of strange people about.' The agent paused and appraised Charles. 'Middle-aged men, possibly not very happy in their private lives, who are often anxious to get in touch with my girls. They are after all, attractive girls.'

'Oh, very attractive.'

'Yes. And I have to protect them. But in the case of Janine any moral decision I might have to make about putting her in touch with you is made for me.'

'What do you mean?'

'I can't put you in touch with her. I don't know where she is.'

'But you must know where the group's working.'

'Janine is no longer a member of the group.'

'When did she leave?'

'Rang me about a week ago. Said she had to get out "for personal reasons". Bloody inconvenient for the group. They've just got a big telly spectacular coming up and I've got plenty on my plate without having to rush around auditioning new girls. Apart from anything else, all the one's I've seen so far have been terrible.'

'So Janine left just at the end of the Hunstanton booking?'

'Exactly.'

'Could you give me her home address so that I can contact her there?'

'Wouldn't do you a lot of good if I did. She's moved out. Used to live in a flat with a boy-friend, but I gather they've split up. Anyway, he's moved out too.'

'You don't know the boy-friend's name?'

'No. I spoke to him once or twice on the phone, but never got his name. Janine kept her private life very private.'

'Oh.' Disappointing. A blind alley.

'Incidentally, Mr . . . Don't tell me your name, because I'm as unlikely to believe that as I am your phoney cover as an insurance salesman . . . I find it rather strange that you know the Foolish Things have just been in Hunstanton.'

Charles smiled feebly. 'Oh, I like to keep an interest in show business.'

'I also find it strange that you asked me for Janine's private address when you told my secretary you'd tried her home. She's lived in the same place for three years.'

'Ah.' The cover was definitely blown. Maybe try the truth. See how that went down. 'Look, in fact I'm a kind of private detective.' Well, a heightened version of the truth. 'I'm investigating a crime and I believe that Janine can help me with some information.'

It did sound melodramatic. Green looked at Charles for a long time, weighing the likelihood of this new story. He appeared to make up his mind. 'I see. Well, I suppose society has a duty to help people like you, though yours is a rather unpleasant business.' He tore a piece of paper off a pad on his desk and wrote something on it. He sealed it in an envelope and wrote on that. 'Go to this address. They may be able to give you what you're looking for.'

Green and his secretary's fascinated stares followed Charles out of the office.

The address was not far away. In Old Compton Street. It was a strip club. Photographs bulged either side of the curtained doorway. It didn't look a likely place to find a missing dancer, but that was where he had been directed.

Inside the doorway Charles was met by a stocky gentleman who looked very familiar. Mr. Green without a nose-job. Must be a brother.

'Can I help you, sir?'

Charles handed over the note. The man tore it open and read it. 'Fine, sir. Well, it may be rather expensive, but I'm sure you'll find it well worth the money. Now, in fact there isn't any film in the cameras, but I think that only adds to the excitement. The girls will move about and pose for you, but I'm afraid we do have to insist on the rule of no touching. Now if you'd like to—'

'What the hell are you talking about? I'm just trying to find Janine.'

'You can call the girls whatever you like. They won't mind. Call one Janine if you—'

'What the hell did it say in that note?' Charles snatched it back and read:

DEAR JOE,
   THIS KINK WAS COMING ROUND SNIFFING AFTER ONE OF MY DANCERS. SEEMS MORE YOUR LINE. WELL IT'S BUSINESS. LOVE TO MYRA AND THE KIDS. MIKE.

Oh dear. He shouldn't have worn that raincoat.

# Chapter V

COMIC: I say, I say, I say, why did the film-mad
    chicken cross the road?
FEED: I don't know. Why did the film-mad
    chicken cross the road?
COMIC: To see Gregory Peck.

'As you can imagine, Gerald, I felt quite a fool.'

'Yes. Of course, if you are going to turn funny,
you're about the right age for it. I mean, if you do feel
you want to start flashing in the park. It's only to be expected.'

'Ha, ha. You're condemning yourself too. You're the
same age as me. And smooth solicitors aren't immune
from developing embarrassing habits. So watch it.'

Gerald chuckled uneasily down the phone. He was
worried that his secretary Polly might be listening in. In
spite of her obvious maturity and worldy eye, he had an
old-fashioned view of what she should be allowed to
hear or see.

Charles continued, 'One thing was interesting. Even
though he did think I was some kind of pervert, the information he gave me was true. Janine and her boy-
friend have recently moved out of their flat. I've
checked.'

'Where did you get the address?'

'Amazingly, from Maurice. You know, Maurice
Skellern, my agent, the theatrical 'Who's Sleeping with

Who'. He knew somebody who knew somebody who had once known Janine. Rang me back within half an hour. He's impressively efficient about everything except being an agent.'

'He didn't know who Janine's boy-friend was?'

'No. Nobody seems to know that. But they've certainly both moved out.'

'If you went to the flat, surely you could have checked with the landlord.'

'I didn't go to the flat. I just rang up and spoke to the new tenants. They didn't know who had been living there before. But I got the landlord's name and rang him. He was, to put it mildly, unhelpful. To put it less mildly, bloody abusive. That's why I rang you.'

'I don't follow.'

'I thought maybe you could use your professional position. If you were to identify yourself and ask him, he'd probably tell you.'

'Hmm.'

'I mean, solicitors carry weight—and not just from all those lunches they have at their client's expense.'

'Ha, ha. You have a very puerile sense of humour, Charles. All right, I'll try and ring you back.'

Gerald fulfilled his promise within ten minutes. 'I understand what you mean about downright abusive.'

'Ah. He didn't tell you anything either?'

'He told me all he knew, but it wasn't very helpful. He didn't even know Janine had been living there. Some bloke had a five-year lease on the place and it's been through a long sequence of sublets—you know, the lease passed on with a payment euphemistically known as "fixtures and fittings". Used to be known as "key money". Illegal, but pretty common, particularly since the Rent Act. It was on the subject of this practice that the landlord became downright abusive.'

'Hmm. So Janine's trail has gone cold?'

'Yes, Charles. For the time being, she's disappeared.'

'Right.'

'Which must surely lend support to your theory that she killed Peaky.'

'Yes. Except, since the inquest raised no suspicion of foul play and she doesn't know that anyone disbelieves its findings, why does she need to disappear?'

'See your point. What elese could it mean, though?'

'Well . . . if someone else murdered Peaky and she found out, then she might know too much and . . . I don't know, it's only conjecture, but the timing does seem odd. There must be some connection between Peaky's death and her disappearance.'

'Sure thing, buster.'

'The main priority is still to find her. And to get as much background on the case as possible. I'll pump Lennie Barber some more.'

'Oh yes, of course, the show's tomorrow. How was the rehearsal?'

'I don't really know. It's more like army drill than rehearsal. Barber gives me my timing by numbers. "I say my line, you give it a count of two, then you come in. In the middle of the speech a count of four and at the end of the line give three before you move your head." I think a computer could be programmed to do it instead of me. And probably better.'

'Is the material funny?'

'God knows. It seems pretty corny to me, but then I'm not an expert on comedy script. Also rehearsing it this way would take the humour out of anything. See how the audience reacts tomorrow night.'

'I'll be out front rooting for you, baby. And, incidentally, anything else I can do for you on the investigation front, just let me know.'

*The Alexander Harvey Show* was prerecorded some four hours before its late-night Saturday transmission, so that any major technical cock-ups or offences against public decency could be edited out. Like most chat shows, it kept its guests in a well-stocked hospitality

room until such time as they were fed out like gladiators
into the arena with Alexander Harvey. The theory was
that a drink would relax the guest into his most
sparkling form. The danger was that the guests could
become relaxed to the point of incoherence and occasionally even fall off their swivel chairs.

Charles was beginning to fear that this might be the
case with Lennie Barber. The comedian had ap-
propriated a whole bottle of whisky from the rather
dishy researcher who was looking after them, and was
working through it as if it were lemonade. Charles who
himself had a modest proficiency with a whisky bottle,
was amazed at the speed with which it was going down.
He was stinting himself for fear of forgetting the
elaborate system of acting by numbers which he had just
learnt, but Lennie Barber seemed to be affected by no
such inhibitions.

'Bloody awful medium, television,' the comedian
mumbled disconsolately. 'No atmosphere, you do
everything a dozen times, keep stopping and starting.
You can't see the bloody audience and they can't see
you for all the cameras and sound booms and bloody
people. So many people around, just hanging around.
Looks as if they're gathering for a lynching.'

'Didn't you like it when you did the old *Barber and
Pole Shows*?'

'It was different then. Less sophisticated. Less bloody
cameras. You just did your act. Now it's all arty-farty.
Still, you got to do it. Never turn up a telly. That's what
people watch these days. Got to be seen if you're going
to make it.'

'Yes, and of course that's where the money is,'
Charles contributed knowledgeably.

'Not the real money. Sure, television's good. But the
real money for a comedian's in cabaret. Those big
cabaret joints, the clubs, they pay the comic all the door
money, virtually. Make their dough on the drinks and
the chicken-in-the-basket. Yes, if you want to clean up,
get on to one of the major cabaret circuits. Mind you,

you need to do the telly for them to book you. Bleedin'
vicious circle.' Lennie Barber morosely refilled his
whisky. His hands were no longer bandaged, no doubt
as a concession to the television camera, but he held the
glass and bottle gingerly. As he put the bottle down,
Charles saw on his palm the bright pink of new skin
surrounded by yellowing flakes which were all that
remained of the blisters.

Lennie Barber's burns were genuine. Which, to
Charles' mind, made it very unlikely that the old
comedian could have killed Bill Peaky.

'Um, I think we'll probably be going ahead in about
ten minutes,' said the dishy researcher, and added for
the seventh time, 'So it'll just be about ten minutes' chat
along the lines Alex suggested and then straight into the
sketch on the special set.'

'Fine. Point me in the right direction when the time
comes,' Barber mumbled slackly.

'Are you sure you feel all right, Mr Barber?' Her
pretty little face looked anxious. Good heavens, was this
show going to be a MAJOR DISASTER to be talked about
for weeks in the bar? Like all girls in their twenties in
television, she took it TERRIBLY SERIOUSLY and she
wasn't sure that she could cope with an incapably drunk
guest. Oh dear, would Alex blame her?

'I'm on top of the world,' Barber's tones were even
more slurred.

'Oh, um. If you'll excuse me, I must just have a word
with the producer.' And she scuttled out, all White Rabbit.

Charles, who had also been worried by the sudden
deterioration in Barber's condition, was relieved to
receive a wink.

'Get 'em worried. They love it in television. Feel lost
without an atmosphere of panic.'

Charles laughed. 'She's a pretty little thing. Your
type?'

'My type?'

'Your type of woman?'

'I haven't got a type of woman any more. Just no interest in them. I've been through it all—affairs, marriage, divorce, one-night stands, little dancers, big landladies, the lot—and now I couldn't give a damn. It's as if all that bit of my life just doesn't exist.'

'But don't you miss it?'

'Never give it a thought. I find, getting older, lots of things that used to be important just don't matter any more. I look back and I think, why the hell did I waste all my time with that?'

'Yes.' Charles mused. In a strange way the moment seemed propitious to continue his inquiries into Bill Peaky's death. With no apologies for the change of subject, he started. 'Lennie, you know you told me about Bill Peaky having an affair with one of the girls in Hunstanton . . .'

'With three of them, yes.'

'But one in particular. Janine.'

'Yes.'

'You've no idea where she is, have you? I want to contact her.'

So far the comedian had not seemed to notice the change in direction of the conversation, but at this he looked up. 'Now why do you want to contact her? Oh, just a minute, Walter told me something about you being a bit of an amateur detective on the quiet. Is that it? You think there may have been something funny about his death?'

'It's possible.'

'The coroner didn't seem to think so.'

'No, but I happen to know that Peaky did test out his equipment as usual that day.'

Barber registered genuine surprise at that. 'How on earth did you find that out?'

'Norman del Rosa saw him. For reasons of his own he didn't want to tell the police.'

'I can guess the reasons of his own. He was off stealing the dancers' knickers.'

'Not far off.'

'So, what . . . you reckon someone fiddled with the electrics after Peaky had tested them?'

'Again, it's possible.'

'But how?'

'Haven't got that far yet.'

'Hmm. I think you may be on a wild goose chase. That theatre's electrics were so ropey nothing would surprise me about them. I would imagine whatever the fault was just came and went.'

'Maybe.'

'But anyway, your suspicions are heading towards Janine at the moment?'

'As she had been having an affair with him and had a major row on the day of his death, she would seem to have some sort of motive.'

'Yes. Mind you, who didn't? I don't think there was a single person in that company whose back he hadn't got up at some point. He was bloody rude to everyone—all the dancers, the pop group lot, that miserable little pianist. Even poor old Walter. He'd been hanging round for some time trying to get a telly show going, but Peaky treated him like dirt, kept saying he was getting better offers from the other companies, that sort of line.'

'Oh, so Walter had been down to see the show before that day?'

'Oh yeah, three or four times.'

'I see. But going back to Janine . . .''

'Sorry. Don't think I can help you. Never even knew her address.'

'She's moved anyway, but I thought you might know some of her friends or . . .'

'Don't know she had any. You could try the rest of the group, I suppose. No, she was a funny little thing. Very quiet. Apparently lived with this boy-friend in London, but nobody never knew his name. I gather the entry of Prince Bloody Charming Bill Peaky into her life really confused her. Should she give up boy-friend? Should she even tell boy-friend? You know how screwed up kids get about that sort of thing.'

He spoke as if people who got upset about sexual matters belonged to an alien race. The whisky glass was filled again and emptied.

Charles was back where he started. Barber's comments had told him nothing new about Janine. They had opened up possibilities for investigation of other characters involved in *Sun 'n' Funtime*, but Charles found it difficult to concentrate on more than one suspect at a time. Until he had seen Janine, any other course of enquiry seemed a bit futile. Once she had been eliminated . . . Even as he thought it, the word 'eliminated' took on sinister overtones. What had happened to Janine Bentley?

The producer of the show arrived with the dishy researcher. Lennie Barber slumped back into his posture of glazed incapacity.

'All set?' asked the producer with imposed joviality. (Incidentally, the producer was not Walter Proud, who, though responsible for the original idea of recreating the Barber and Pole routine, seemed since to have been pushed into the background.)

'Set? I'm as set as a bloody blancmange, thank you.' Lennie Barber rose to his feet expansively, then seemed to lose his balance and sank back, arms windmilling, on to the side of his chair. Chair and comedian collapsed in a sprawling heap on the floor. The producer and the dishy researcher hastened forward to scoop Barber up.

'Are you going to be all right for the show?' The acid in the producer's tone was trickling straight down to his stomach to feed his incipient ulcer.

'No problem.' Lennie Barber oriented himself towards the door and got through it, hardly hitting the frame at all.

Ignoring Charles, the producer and the dishy researcher scuttled after. As they passed, he heard them muttering, 'Thank God we keep that interview with Greg Robson in reserve. Just need a quick announcement from continuity about a change to the scheduled programme.'

Alexander Harvey's high viewing figures did not exactly reflect his personal popularity. Indeed, many of the people who watched the programme did so merely to confirm how much they disliked him. Being the host on a chat-show is, by its nature, a thankless task, because everyone tunes in to see the guests rather than the presenter anyway, and the host has the options of either keeping a profile low to the point of anonymity or high to the point of irritation. Alexander Harvey had chosen the latter course.

Sometimes this paid handsome dividends. He was very good at stimulating the reticent and cutting short the long-winded, and often the guests, in sheer exasperation at the manner of his questioning, made newsworthy indiscretions. Also he was clever—no one denied that—and was quick at picking up nuances or spotting potentially interesting new directions for the conversation.

His approach also had disadvantages. Apart from the obvious one that the viewing public, who didn't basically like him, were constantly having their attention drawn back to him, he sometimes tended to cut short an interviewee too early into an anecdote and not to allow his victims to pace the conversation to their own style.

He was also 'very into' The Arts and considered his guests on a sliding scale of esoteric snobbery. Opera stars he held in highest esteem, breathing adulation over them with every word. Other classical musicians got a fairly high rating. Theatrical knights and dames scored well, though the rest of the acting profession came rather lower down the scale. Authors and playwrights were OK, so long as they weren't too successful with the public. Popular singers had to have unexpected sidelines to rate anything other than contempt. And comedians . . . Well, comedians were there to be patronised with ill-disguised disgust.

Though that was the basic outline of his scale of values, there were other variables which made predictions of his treatment of a guest difficult. For instance, Hollywood cast a special glow. Any performer, however terrible, who had appeared in some black-and-white 'B' feature in the forties and who could drop the names of a couple of superannuated directors, immediately shot up the league. Being American also improved the credit rating. And being old was an enormous asset. The older the better. Old people gave Alexander Harvey the opportunity to show (a) How good he was with old people; (b) How well he (or in fact one of his researchers) had researched his guest's career; and (c) How important Alexander Harvey was to have such venerable figures chatting to him in such a convivial manner.

So to receive optimum treatment on the *Alexander Harvey Show* a guest should be a hundred-year-old American opera singer who had made a lot of Hollywood films in the course of a long and anecdote-littered career.

Exactly where all this left Lennie Barber, Charles was not certain, but everything pointed to a patronising roasting. The only plus point the comedian had on the Alexander Harvey scale was age, and he didn't really have that in sufficient quantity. Lennie Barber was only sixty-two and Alexander Harvey came into his own with octagenarians and nonagenarians. And, Charles discovered from the dishy researcher, Barber also suffering a big minus—he had been someone else's idea. It should have been mentioned that the ideal hundred-year-old opera singer must have been suggested for the show by Alexander Harvey himself.

Charles lurked round the back of the set as the interview started and watched events on a black-and-white monitor. It was clear from his first words that Alexander Harvey was in a carving-up mood. His introduction was couched in a camp sneer. He gave exactly the sort of information that Barber would have hated. '. . . whom you may remember from the forties and fifties when he was very successful in the apprentice days of television. Unfortunately, with the death of Wilkie Pole, the act was over and public taste seemed to change. However we are delighted to say that he is still a working comedian and it's a great privilege for me to welcome tonight—Mr Lennie Barber!'

From his vantage point Charles could see both sides of Barber's entry. The reeling approach behind the flats (for the benefit of the producer's coronary and the dishy researcher's hot flushes) and the upright dignified appearance on camera (for the benefit of the viewing public).

The studio audience's applause was surprisingly warm. In spite of the changes time had wrought, they still found Lennie Barber comfortingly familiar, like cups of Ovaltine and ration books and tram tickets and suspender belts, a link with a simpler time.

But it was clear as Alexander Harvey came in over the applause that he was out for blood. 'Now, Lennie, you're a comedian, you have been one all your life, you must have thought a lot about the nature of comedy, so tell me. . . .' He paused ingenuously. It was clever. He was going to get the comedian to talk about the nature of comedy, knowing that analysis of humour reduces intelligent people to incoherent wafflers and brilliant comedians to unfunny bores. This was an ideal start for the Alexander Harvey method. His victim was bound to go on at inordinate length, until an incisive interruption from Harvey would point up his long-windedness. The question was poised delicately in the air. 'What makes a joke funny?'

'An audience laughing at it,' Lennie Barber replied immediately, and by doing so, proved that he had just made a joke. The audience laughed. The line itself wasn't funny, but Barber's speed of delivery and obvious contempt for the question, coupled with Harvey's expression of surprise, made it a very funny moment.

Alexander Harvey was disconcerted to the point of looking at the notes on his clipboard (something which usually happened much later into one of his interviews). He had to come in quickly with another question. The longer the break after Barber's reply, the longer the comedian's triumph. But Harvey was a professional and he shaped his next question skilfully. He asked something which would make Barber define his own success or failure. 'You've been a comedian all your life and comedy is a notoriously insecure profession. One day you're on top, the next nobody wants to know about you. When in your career did you feel really confident that you had made it?'

'Tuesday nights mostly.' Again the response was perfectly timed and the audience picked up the sexual innuendo instantly.

Alexander Harvey's mouth hardened into a little line of petulance. These short answers may have been to the audience's taste, but they made it difficult for him to impose his own rhythm on the interview. He decided to slow the proceedings down and reassert control with a longer question.

'One thing I must ask you—we hear constantly about the issues of censorship and permissiveness.' (He was trying to steer Barber into an area of serious discussion where the comedian would show himself up as trivial.) 'Now, the traditions of the music hall are very robust, even vulgar—I suppose I'm thinking of people like Marie Lloyd, Max Miller. When you were in the double act with Wilkie Pole, your material was very clean, but now that a lot of the taboos are down and you are still working in the comedy field, how do you view sex?'

'Through binoculars.' Prompt again, right on cue. Alexander Harvey was being reduced to the level of a feed and the more he tried to take control, the more he set himself up.

He laughed insincerely and pressed on with his next question as if this badinage was all very well, but not really what the public had switched on to see. 'Now, Lennie, there's a cliché around that comedians are pretty pathetic people offstage . . .'

'Some of them are pretty pathetic onstage.' The audience roared again.

'I mean that, as in the example of Pagliacci,' (Hoping to show Barber up by abstruse reference) 'clowns are essentially tragic figures—do you subscribe to this view?'

'I don't know. What's the subscription?' (Laughter).

'What I mean is that comedians yearn to be taken seriously. For instance, they're supposed to have aspirations towards the legitimate theatre. Do you want to play Hamlet?'

'What at?' (Laughter.)

'Ha, ha, very good. Perhaps we could move on to television. I mean, here you are, a comedian brought up through the tough school of the music hall, which is now dead, and here we are on today's medium, television. It has been said that music hall died and television was the box they put it in—do you agree with that?'

'What, that people on television are dead?' (Laughter.)

'No, no.'

'I'm sorry. I've been watching too many chat-shows.' (Laughter and applause.)

'Yes. I'm sorry. I was trying to ask a serious question.' Harvey sounded as piqued as the local favourite beaten for the Women's Institute Flower Arranging Trophy by a complete novice. 'Let me try another tack. It always seems to me that it must be difficult for a comedian to have any dignity. I . . . er . . .'

Alexander Harvey paused for a second, apparently perplexed. He could see the Floor Manager beyond the circle of light gesturing at him. The man was circling his hand in the accepted 'wind-up' signal. Time to bring the chat to an end. What threw Alexander Harvey was that, though he had seen the signal any number of times, he had never actually seen it while he was talking. It was

usually while some nonagenarian flautist was telling a
rambling tale about Sir Thomas Beecham. But now it
was being directed at him. His confusion came with the
realisation that he was the one who was being boring,
that he was the one whom the director was no doubt
vilifying in the control room. He stumbled in his sentence and then picked up momentum with an edge of
bitchiness. 'Um, Marty Feldman once said that comedy
was an unnatural act—would you agree?'

'Would I agree to an unnatural act? Is that a
proposition?' asked Lennie Barber coolly and perfectly.
The audience erupted into laughter and applause. Barber's riposte had struck a chord in all of them. Not only
had it been rude to a man whom at bottom they hated; it
had also reflected their own suspicions about his sexual
identity.

Alexander Harvey, a fixedly indulgent smile on his
face, hastily gestured at his guest, to make it look as if
he was cueing the applause rather than letting it arise
spontaneously. But the gesture was too late. There was
no doubt that, at the end of the contest, Lennie Barber
had won by a knockout.

Alexander Harvey linked ungraciously into the
sketch, but he could no longer do any harm. Snide re-
marks about 'the sort of comedy that used to be popular
in the late thirties' could not weaken Barber's hold on
his audience. And the omission of Charles Paris' name
from his introduction was unlikely to worry anyone except Frances (bound to be watching), Maurice Skellern
(possibly ill with excitement at the thought of one of his
clients actually being in work) and, of course, Charles
himself.

After the interview, the sketch could not fail. The
script was really pretty limp stuff, containing every old
barbershop joke that ever groaned into life. But audiences like old jokes, and Lennie Barber was the hero
of the hour. Apart from that, he rose above his material. Charles, as he went through his automation acting routine ('Be pardon —1—2—3—Bepardon?') found

his respect for the comedian soaring. Lennie Barber was right; he did know how comedy worked.

The set-up of the sketch was simple. Barber, in a hastily-assumed white coat, was the barber. Wilkie Pole was a gormless North Country youth who was about to meet his girl and wanted a quick hair-cut and shave 'so's I look me best, like, for me little girlie—1—2—(Bashful simper).' Barber, having offered him 'hair-cuts, hair-brushes, hair-combs, hair-oil, hair-tonic, hair-restorer—sounds like a German picnic, doesn't it?', sat him in the chair and proceeded to hack away at the special wig on his head, keeping up a running stream of gags the while. When the wig was reduced to a haystack he started on the shaving. He kept cutting his client's chin ('Only a little nick, sir.') and putting pieces of paper on the cuts. Pole left the shop with his face a mass of confetti and his hair in shreds.

The jokes were equally simple. For example, Barber would be stropping his razor. 'Always get it very sharp, sir, got to be sharp. I test my razors by seeing if they can cut through a single hair. A single hair.' (HE SUDDENLY WHIPS A PROP HARE OUT OF HIS COAT AND SLASHES AT IT WITH THE RAZOR, WHICH HAS NO EFFECT.) 'Not sharp enough.' (HE CONTINUES STROPPING.)

Or again . . .

BARBER: And now for the lather . . . Only the finest shaving brush is used. Genuine ivory stem. Do you realise an an elephant gave his life just so that you could look elegant for your girlie?

POLE: Ooh.

BARBER: Not to mention the badger.

POLE: The badger?

BARBER (PUSHING THE SHAVING BRUSH INTO HIS MOUTH): I told you not to mention the badger. And then of course there's the shaving soap. I have a great variety of shaving soaps. How would you like your shaving soap?

POLE: Oh, I'd like it scented.

BARBER: No, it's much easier if you take it with you.

But what you really need is my very own special soap.
It's a mixture of silver paint and sulphuric acid and it
has two advantages—first, it means you can see your
face in your chin so you don't need a mirror. And
second, you get some amazing dimples.

And third . . . it makes the lather go farther.

This last line was greeted by an enormous round of
applause. It was one of the old Barber and Pole catch-
phrases. That, along with 'It helps the soap to cope',
'Only a little nick, sir' and 'Bepardon?' were all the
trade-marks of the double act. And the audience clung
to them like religion in an age of uncertainty. They
responded ecstatically.

Even the hardware of a television studio failed to ruin
the atmosphere. Because the moves and action of the
sketch were so fixed, it had been possible to make the
camera script very simple. The whole six minutes ran
without break and no retakes were required.

There was no doubt about it. The show had been an
enormous success.

Charles stood by the bar at the back of the scrum of
television people getting drinks. He felt strange and
needed the reassurance of a large Bell's.

It was such a long time since he had felt that kind of
warmth from an audience. Such a long time since he had
appeared in anything more than modestly successful. To
his annoyance, he felt rather emotional. It was a moving
experience to feel the response of a wildly enthusiastic
audience. It cut through all his layers of cynicism and
left him exposed like a stagestruck teenager.

'Drink, drink, old boy. Really terrific show. There's
the beginning of something here, or the old nose for success has got its sinuses blocked.' Walter Proud's
bonhomous arm was flung round his shoulders. 'Sid.
Sid.' The producer waved at the barman. 'What's it to
be, Charles?'

'Large Bell's, please.'

'Of course, of course. Should have remembered. That's a large Bell's, Sid, and my usual, a large gin with . . .' But the barman's attention was elsewhere. 'Look, I think I was first. Excuse me, Charles, I must just . . .' Walter dived into the mêlée.

'Not bad. Thank you.' Charles turned to see Lennie Barber behind him and took the brusque words as a great compliment. The comedian was not given to sycophancy.

'I'm very grateful to you for all your help, Lennie. As I said, it's a completely new field for me. I've found it fascinating. And may I say how marvellous I thought you were with Alexander Harvey. And in the sketch . . . really great.' Oh dear, is there nothing that one performer can say to another that doesn't sound insincere?

'He's nothing, that Harvey, after you've played a second house in Liverpool.'

The subject of their conversation approached with a smile sculpted on to his face and a hand outstretched. 'Lovely show. Delighted with it. I hope I set them all up for you all right,' he added jocularly, as if his discomfiture had been part of a subtle master plan.

Lennie Barber looked at Alexander Harvey seriously before replying. Then, as if he had thought it out in some detail, he said, 'You weren't that good actually, lad. Tell you what, you do three or four years round the clubs and you might turn into a reasonable feed.'

A visible effort of will kept the smile in place on the face of the country's most popular chat-show host. While he searched his mental quiver for a barb with sufficient poison on it to use in reply, he was interrupted by the arrival behind him of a neat forty-year-old man in a grey suit.

'Very nice show, Alex,' congratulated the newcomer. 'Thought it went very well.'

'Oh thanks,' said a rather deflated Alexander Harvey.

At that moment Walter Proud bustled up with

Charles' Bell's and his own gin. He greeted the man in the grey suit effusively. 'Nigel, great to see you. How goes it?'

'Fine, fine,' said the man in the grey suit.

'You haven't got a drink. What is it? Still the Campari?'

'That'd be very nice, thank you.'

'What about you, Alex? Lennie? Actually, Nigel, when I've got the drinks, I'd like to bend your ear for a moment about a couple of ideas.'

'Fine, fine.' The man grinned vaguely as Walter disappeared into the bar scrum, then turned sharply to Alexander Harvey. 'Who is that?'

'Walter Proud. Used to be at the BBC.'

'Oh yes, I've met him somewhere. He's not with us at the moment, is he?'

'Yes, three months' contract. Meant to be coming up with ideas. Tonight was one of his.' Alexander Harvey grimaced.

'I see. I've got to go and talk to Paul over there. Excuse me.' The man in the grey suit flicked Charles and Barber a professional smile and moved away with Alexander Harvey in tow.

Charles looked at the comedian quizzically. 'He's Nigel Frisch, Director of Programmes here and one very important person.'

Walter emerged from the scrum of drinks. 'Oh, where did they go to?' He handed a very large Scotch to Barber who pointed to the other side of the bar. 'I'll take the drinks over. You know, Lennie, I'm really excited by what happened tonight. I think we're on to something. I think we can get a show going, built round the old Barber and Pole routines—I mean, not just old stuff, get in some young writers, you know give it a bit of edge, kind of revue format—we'd be on to a winner. It wouldn't be just the nostalgia appeal, though that's there. I reckon if you can present the public with a package that's got nostalgia and is modern at the same time, then you've got to be on to a winner. Lennie Barber, I think you could be on the verge of the biggest comeback there ever was. Well, what do you say?'

Lennie Barber shrugged without changing his expression. 'I say "Oh yeah?" '

'Yeah. Certainly.'

'Show me the contract and I might believe you.'

'Well, at least sound a bit excited about it.'

'If I got excited every time I heard a producer say I was on the verge of a comeback, I'd have dropped dead years ago. Once you've been an overnight success more than a couple of dozen times the novelty wears off.'

'This time it's for real. This one's going to be big.'

'Yeah, sure.' Barber spoke as to a child. 'You go and take those drinks over to your important friends.' As Walter moved away, the comedian downed his Scotch in a single gulp.

'Get you another one, Lennie?'

'No, Charles. I haven't got the cash with me to buy you one.'

'Well, I can get it now, or lend you the money or—'

'Don't like being in debt, sorry. No, I'll go and join that little group over there round the director. Since I'm going to appear on the bugger's expense claim whether he buys me a drink or not, I think he can get me one.'

Charles stood alone and drank. His mind kept coming back to Janine Bentley. Pretty girl. Long golden hair. Not an intelligent face, but a sweet one. Appealing, childish really. Where was she?

'Look, I do want to talk about the series potential in this thing, Charles old man.' It was Walter back again. Nigel Frisch and Alexander Harvey had only required him as a waiter for their drinks and had not volunteered to include him in their conversation.

Charles' mind was not on series potential. 'Walter, you know that show at Hunstanton . . . ?'

'Yes.'

'You saw it a few times, I gather?'

'Yes.' Walter looked at him blankly.

'Did you meet one of the dancers called Janine?'

The producer's look changed from blankness to slight suspicion. 'Yes, I met her.'

'Apparently she was having an affair with Bill Peaky.'

'Yes, or he was with her, whichever way you like to put it. So what? Do you disapprove?'

'No, no. It's just . . . I don't know, they're supposed to have had a quarrel on the afternoon he died.'

'Yes, somebody mentioned that. She was serious about him; he wasn't about her. Apparently Janine had been in touch with Peaky's wife and told her what was going on, imagining, I think, that the wife would give up her claims and allow the course of true love to run smooth.'

'Really. And that's what annoyed Peaky?'

'I gather so. It'd annoy most men. I'd have been pretty damned annoyed if any of my little bits on the side had told Angela.' Somehow the sexual bravado in his tone didn't carry conviction.

'Hmm. Do you know what Peaky's relationship with his wife was?'

'Well, they were married. Sorry, being facetious. I don't know. I think OK, but Bill used to put it about a bit.'

'So I heard. Incidentally, Walter, do you know Peaky's wife—widow, I should say?'

'I've met her. Carla. Pretty girl. Lives out towards Epping Forest somewhere. Wouldn't say I know her really.' Walter Proud drained his gin reflectively. 'Pity about Bill Peaky. Really talented boy. I thought I'd get some kind of show going there. Still, it's an ill wind. If I hadn't gone to Hunstanton to see him, I wouldn't have made contact with old Lennie Barber again and tonight wouldn't have happened.'

Gerald Venables, who had been ensconced in a corner of the bar with the head of the television company's contract department, offered to drive Charles home.

'So where do you go now, big boy?' he asked as the Mercedes purred along.

'I reckon finding Janine is still the first priority.'

'Cherchez la femme.'

'But since the trail seems to have gone cold there at the moment, I think I might cherchez the family instead for a bit.'

'Whose family?'

'Peaky's family. I think I'll get in touch with his widow.'

## Chapter VI

COMIC: Do you know, I'm going to marry a
widow.
FEED: Are you? Ooh, I wouldn't fancy being the
second husband of a widow.
COMIC: I'd sooner be the second than the first.

Charles rang the phone number Walter Proud had given
him the next morning. He asked to speak to Mrs Peaky
and was told he was speaking to Mrs Pratt, who was Bill
Peaky's widow. He should have realised that Peaky was
too good a name for a comedian to be genuine.

He had decided that when he spoke to her, he would
not attempt any subterfuge. Since she had not been in
Hunstanton at the time, she could not possibly have
been implicated in her husband's death and she was
likely to be interested to hear of any suspicious circumstances.

She spoke slowly, treading her accent with caution
like a tight-rope walker, all right at her own pace, but at
speed in danger of falling into the Cockney below.
'What's it about?'

'You don't know me, Mrs Pratt, and I hope you
don't mind my calling you. My name's Charles Paris. I
was present in Hunstanton when your husband died.'

'Yes?'

'I'm sorry. I don't want to upset you, but I've since

heard things that make me wonder whether his death was in fact an accident.'

'Whether it was . . . What, you mean that someone might have . . . that he might have been murdered?'

'I believe it's possible.'

There was a long pause from the other end of the phone. When it came back, her voice was strained, less at pains to hide its origins. 'Do you have any suspicions as to who might have murdered him?'

'Suspicions, vague thoughts, nothing concrete. I wanted to talk to you about it.'

'Me? But I—'

'I'm sorry. Please don't misunderstand me. Of course I'm not wishing to imply any suspicion of you. I just wanted to talk to you about your husband, ask if you know of anyone with a sufficiently strong grudge against him to . . . I'm sorry, I thought you would be interested.'

'Yes, of course I am. It's just a bit of a shock. I mean, it never occurred to me that . . . You're convinced that it was murder?'

'Fairly convinced, yes.'

'As I say, it's a shock.'

'Of course. Can we meet?'

'I think we should.'

'Just say where and when.'

'Do you mind coming out here? I'm sorry, it's difficult to park the children at short notice. Can you come today?'

Charles' professional calendar was as empty as usual. 'Certainly. Tell me how to get to you.'

There was no evidence of the children when he arrived at the house. Presumably Carla Pratt had managed to park them at short notice after all.

The house was in Chigwell, a nice area for an East End boy like Bill Peaky to aspire to when he started to make a bit of money. No doubt all the neighbours were company directors, professional footballers and minor racketeers. The building was a bungalow that seemed to have sprawled out of control, with a double garage and hacienda-style archways that had been added to take the curse off its thirties redbrick lines. The frontage was all wrought iron, black wrought iron gates relieving black wrought iron railings.

This motif was continued inside the sitting room where black wrought iron supported glass shelves, plant pots, light fittings, marble-topped tables and a series of photographs of Bill Peaky's triumphs. The curled black metal gave the room a coldness, a newness, as if the decor were for show, not for living in.

Carla Pratt was also dressed in black, but she had a higher cuddlability rating than the wrought iron. Her curves were less machined and warmer. Charles had seen her distantly at the inquest, but never without a coat and so had not appreciated her splendid contours. He recalled Walter Proud saying she had been a dancer and child-bearing had not slackened the athleticism of her figure. Nor did the black glazed cotton dress, worn presumably as a token of mourning, do anything to disguise her shape. Indeed, it offered fascinating grounds for conjecture as to whether she was wearing one of those negligible bras made of flimsy stuff like they wrap supermarket chickens in, or none at all.

Her blonde hair had been recently (and expensively) cut and she looked fit and lively. If she was suffering from the pains of widowhood, she disguised it well.

Having sat Charles down and provided him with a cup of coffee (instant, but one of the more expensive blends), she asked him to give his grounds for suspicion and he ran through the business of Norman del Rosa's revelation again.

'That doesn't prove murder,' she said with what sounded like relief. Presumably someone who has just reconciled herself to her husband's death is not anxious to have to change her whole pattern of thinking on the subject.

'Doesn't prove it, but it does make the death seem

rather odd. The particular electrical set-up which caused
it would have been bound to show up on the ringmain
tester.'

'So you think someone fiddled with the wires after
Bill tested it?'

'That would seem a logical conclusion.'

'Hmm.' She seemed to be waiting for him in some
way, waiting for him to come to the point. Maybe she
still feared that he was building up to an accusation.
'But why? Why should anyone do that?'

'One of my reasons for wanting to see you was the
hope that you might be able to answer that question.
The old "Did your husband have any enemies?"
routine.'

'I see. Let me think.' It didn't take her long. 'No, I
don't think so.'

'You mean everyone liked him?'

'Yes.' She looked directly at Charles, as if daring him
to challenge her assertion.

He had no intention of challenging it, but it seemed
odd. This certainly did not tally with what everyone
else had said about Peaky. Still, Carla was his widow.
Maybe in her eyes he could do no wrong. And, of
course, she had not been in the company with him to
hear his slights against fellow-performers.

"But, Mrs Pratt, someone who has as much success
as your husband, and so quickly, is likely to cause
jealousy among other people in the business. Didn't you
ever hear of that sort of thing?'

'Not in Bill's case, no.' She said it with great determination. Difficult to tell whether or not she was
protesting too much. Feeling that maybe she had not
made her point, she added, 'He was a wonderful man.'

Charles lowered his eyes and regretted that he had
never had the pleasure of meeting the young comedian.
'So you can't imagine anyone wanting to get him out of
the way?'

'No. No one except a maniac or someone like that.

Why should anyone in their right mind want to destroy our lives, leave the two boys without their Dad, leave me a widow? It's madness.' She didn't look particularly ruffled as she delivered this speech, but it could have come from genuine feeling. Emotion is revealed in many ways. Charles felt an indefinable suspicion as to her sincerity but decided that he was being hypersensitive.

'I agree, it is madness, Mrs Pratt, but if it were murder, would you mind my investigating it?'

'How'd you mean?'

'I mean, do you want me to find out all I can about the circumstances or would you rather I forgot all about it?'

'No. If there is some possibility that he was murdered, I'd have to know. I mean, if I said forget it, it'd sound like I didn't care.'

'Only to me. No one else would know.'

'That's true.' She vacillated. 'But no, we've got to find out. I loved him. I've got to know.'

Her final avowal again sounded pedestrian, but maybe that was as emotional as she ever got.

Still, she had given Charles a cue and he was obliged to pick it up. 'You say you loved him. You mean it was a happy marriage?'

'Of course,' she snapped.

'I'm sorry to ask you this, but I've talked to other members of the Hunstanton company and they have suggested that perhaps your husband was not always . . . completely faithful?'

He was fully prepared to get his face slapped for that, but her reply was surprisingly mild. 'He was away a lot. I suppose in the nature of things he must have met other girls, had the occasional fling. I never asked. At least he had the decency to keep that sort of thing away from his own doorstep.'

'He never talked about any girl-friends?'

'No. We had a good marriage.' Her persistence on this point was again unsettling. If the marriage was that good, if she had been so desolated by her husband's death, how could she be so cool and collected and even sexy (yes, definitely sexy) so soon afterwards?

'And you never met any of his girl-friends?'

'Never. He wouldn't humiliate me. It was a good marriage,' she insisted.

'Yes. Of course. So the name Janine Bentley doesn't mean anything to you?'

She shook her head. Charles elaborated. 'Janine Bentley is a dancer. She was in the Hunstanton company. Backstage gossip said she was having an affair with your husband just before he died. Backstage gossip also said they had a serious row on the afternoon of his death.'

'What? And you think she might have murdered him out of spite?' Carla asked with wonderment.

Charles shrugged. 'It's a theory. I'd certainly like to talk to her. Unfortunately she's disappeared.'

'But she's your main suspect?'

'I wouldn't say that, but she seems to have had more motive than anyone else. Also opportunity. If I found out something more which pointed to her guilt, I'd be prepared to be very suspicious.'

'I see.' Carla Pratt seemed to be thinking something out. When she spoke again, it was with much greater fluency. Maybe now for the first time she felt that she was not under suspicion and could speak freely. 'I think I have heard of her.'

'From Bill?'

'In a way.'

'I heard a rumour that she was very serious about him. Talking about marriage, expecting him to divorce you, that sort of thing.'

'Bill would never have divorced me.'

'You sound almost as if you wish he had.'

The wistfulness of its tone had given her remark that flavour, but she bridled strongly at the suggestion. 'Certainly not. You got me all wrong if you think that. All I ever wanted was to go on being with Bill. It was a very good marriage.'

'Yes, I'm sorry. I was being facetious. Going back to Janine. The rumours I heard suggested that the row she had with your husband on the afternoon of his death was caused by her threat to tell you about their relationship.'

Carla Pratt was silent for a long time after this. When she did speak, for the first time in their conversation her voice was a little unsteady with emotion. 'You seem to know so much, I might as well tell you.'

Charles made a sympathetic grunt, unwilling to break her new confidential mood with words.

'She did tell me. She rang up here. About a week before Bill died. She said they were having this affair and they wanted to get married and I ought to know.'

'What did you say?'

'I didn't believe her. I mean, I believed Bill was having a bit of fun with her—he liked girls—but nothing serious, no. So after she'd spoken, I rang him and asked. He admitted the affair, but he said she had got it all out of proportion. Apparently she was very mixed-up. Strange kid, a bit unbalanced, so Bill said. Certainly she sounded it when she talked to me.'

'What did she say?'

'She talked about men. Other men she had known. How they'd all been bastards until she met Bill. Apparently she'd had some long affair with a guy in a rock group, trailing round the country, following his tours. That had turned sour. She sounded sort of manic, if that's the word.' As Carla Pratt talked, her posh accent was eroded and the Cockney showed through.

'Did she make any threats against Bill—or indeed against you?'

'No. If she had, I daresay I'd have thought about it when he died and put two and two together.' The last word came out as 'togevver'.

'You didn't have any further contact with her?'

'None at all. She was really weird on the phone, sort of spooky, like people in those exorcism films.'

'And you've no idea where she is now? As I say, she's disappeared.'

'Haven't a clue. Never even met her. Only spoke to her the once. And you know, now I come to think of it, after I come off the phone from talking to her, I felt really frightened.'

As the Underground slowly took him back into central London, Charles went through the interview in his mind. It was full of strange inconsistencies. Carla's image of her husband seemed so at variance with everyone else's. Still, marriage must involve a degree of blindness to the partner's faults. Perhaps it was natural enough. So, come to think of it, was her initial fear that Charles was suspicious of her as her husband's killer. However illogical, everyone's first instinct is to feel guilty. And no doubt her poised sexy exterior was just a carefully built up bastion against uncontrollable emotion.

More important than the contradiction in Carla Pratt's character was the illumination she had given into the character of Janine Bentley. He had had difficulty visualising the girl as a calculating killer. Other descriptions had suggested a rather anonymous, quiet little thing.

But a girl who sounded unbalanced, indeed a girl who would make the kind of phone-call described, was a much more disturbing proposition. And there was another important detail—a girl who had spent a lot of time trailing round after a rock group would pick up some sort of knowledge of how their equipment worked and might well know how to stage a fatal 'accident'.

It was even more imperative that he should find Janine Bentley.

## Chapter VII

COMIC: Did you hear about the Irish tap dancer?
FEED: No.
COMIC: He fell in the sink.

Charles thought it would be tempting providence to approach Mr Mike Green (he who conducted business under an assumed nose) in another disguise. The raincoat débâcle had dealt a blow to his faith in his protean abilities.

Vocally, though, he retained his confidence and it was the perky voice he had used in *Fings Ain't What They Used To Be* ('The boldness of choosing this piece was not justified by the company's abilties.'—*Leamington Spa Courier*) that was transferred through by the suspicious secretary to Mr Green.

'Hello. You say you are from *The Sun*?'

'That's right. Bob Cherry of Photographic Features department.' Oops. Silly choice of name.

But fortunately Mr Green did not seem to be a reader of the Billy Bunter stories. 'I see. What can I do for you?'

'Idea came up at an editorial meeting for doing a series of features on dance groups—gather you represent These Foolish Things—wonder if I could contact the group, have a bit of a chat, background stuff, then if the idea seems to be working send along a photographer, take a few pics. Any objections in principle?'

'No, not in principle, no. When would you want to do this?'

' 'Fraid it's a bit of a rush job—want to get something rough mapped out today, so that the editor can run his peepers over it, give us the go-ahead on the series.'

'Hmm. It might be difficult today. The boys and girls are in rehearsal at the moment.'

Charles took a risk. 'Oh well, if it's not convenient, never mind. I've got a long list of other dance groups drawn up. Thank you for your time.'

'No, no, just a minute.' As Charles had hoped, the lure of publicity in the national press was too strong. 'Look, I'm sure they could take a break for a quick chat. Wouldn't be long, would it?'

'Quarter of an hour top-weight.'

'Fine. Then I'll tell you where they are rehearsing. It's—just a minute there is one thing.'

'Yes?'

'About these photographs . . . I know your paper has a reputation for rather . . . frank pictures. I hope that wasn't the sort of thing you had in mind. I mean, they're lovely girls and that, but the appeal of the group has to be universal. Family audience stuff, they've been booked for kids' telly shows, that sort of thing. Don't want the image let down. They're not your topless go-go dancers, it's a more artistic thing altogether.''

'Of course,' Charles soothed. 'No, this isn't a Page Three feature. Sort of light-weight serious piece on how groups start and get formed and so on.'

'Ah, if you're going to ask them that sort of thing, perhaps I ought to be there.'

Boobed again. 'No, I don't think that'll be necessary. Very straight-forward stuff, not trying to get any angle.'

'I see. Oh, that should be all right. When's it likely to be in the paper?'

'Can't say exactly, I'm afraid, chum. As I say, just a mock-up we're working on at the moment—Editor's bound to give the go-ahead, though—next couple of weeks, I should think.'

'OK.' Mr Green gave the address of the rehearsal room, a police gymnasium in Herne Hill. 'I'll give them a buzz to say you're coming.'

'Oh, you needn't,' said Charles hastily, seeing himself committed to continuing his enquiries in the same identity.

But there was no escape. 'Yes, I'd better. Then there'll be no problem about their letting you in. Get some funny types hanging round the girls, you know. Bob . . . Cherry did you say the name was?''

Charles confirmed it, blushing on two counts. First for the choice of name and second for the reference to funny types hanging round the girls. 'Right. Well, thank you very much for the help, Mr Green.'

'My pleasure . . . By the way, if you ever are looking for girls for the more . . . adult sort of features you do, I might be able to put you in touch with a very useful agency for the . . . less inhibited sort of mode.'

Touting for more work for brother Joe's end of the business, Charles reflected, as he rang off.

He was a bit worried about approaching the group in his new identity (particularly on police premises) but his fears were unfounded. Mr Green's call had prepared the ground well and the dancers' vanity that someone from the Press was interested in them precluded any doubts about his authenticity.

They gathered round at one end of the gymnasium, the girls sitting on low benches with their legs stretched out on the floor and the boys in sculptured poses with hands on hips.

The girls were a great disappointment in rehearsal clothes. Onstage in Hunstanton, even in the publicity photographs he'd seen, he wouldn't have kicked any of them out of bed, but seeing them here, he felt that his feet might be more actively employed. Their leotards and bulky leg-warmers did not do a lot for their figures, creating the impression of a randomly-lagged water system in the loft of an old house. Their faces were testimonials to the skill of modern make-up and hair-dressing. With the paint scoured off and hair swept back into rubber bands, they looked like peeled grapes. In spite of his long experience of the Jekyll and Hyde propensities of actresses, Charles still found it a shock.

Interviewing them was not difficult. Like most performers, they needed little prompting to talk about themselves. The difficulty Charles found was in pretending to be interested in their anecdotes of early promise and not rushing on to the questions he really wanted to ask.

But after eight histories of stage school, ballet lessons, studio dance training and unsuccessful attempts at acting in musicals, he managed to ask how long they had all been together.

The tallest boy, who posed like a pampas grass in a fireplace and acted as spokesman, replied. 'Ooh, about eighteen months now. Leonie and I came from The Best Thing, Wayne and Darryl were with the Black and White Minstrels, Polly, Boots and Cookie were from a little set-up called The Tootsies, and . . . er, Barbie is straight out of Italia Conti.'

The last-named looked less like a poulterer's wares than the other girls. She was probably only seventeen, but the dark circles under her eyes bespoke more than a nodding acquaintance with the endless round of rehearsals and performances. She was the one unfamiliar face in the group, obviously Janine Bentley's replacement.

'Have you had your hair done differently?' Bob Cherry asked ingenuously. 'I've seen publicity photos of the group and I'm sure you used to look different.'

'Wasn't me, I've only just joined last week.'

'What happened to the other girl?' Bob Cherry asked casually.

'She left for personal reasons,' supplied the tallest boy.

'What does that mean?'

'Just what it says. Nothing to do with the group. No quarrel or anything.'

'I think she'd been having boy-friend trouble,' supplied the girl called Cookie. 'Been having a rough time for a few months. I think she left because she wanted a bit of time to get her head together.

'Ah.' Charles wouldn't liked to have defined exactly what that meant, but he thought he got the gist of it. 'Any idea how I can contact her?'

'She's left the group. Not much point in contacting her, really,' the tallest boy insisted, seeing the available publicity about to be divided nine ways instead of eight.

'Sure, but as I say this article's about how groups are made up. It would be a great help if I could find her and have a chat.'

'She won't tell you anything shocking or awful. As I say, there wasn't any quarrel.'

'No, no, it's not a muck-raking article. I'm not after that sort of thing. When did she leave you?'

'Just after we finished our summer season in Hunstanton, couple of weeks back.'

'Be a pity if I couldn't contact her. Talking to an ex-member of the group would add that little something to the article, sort of extra dimension the Editor always wants. Without something different, who knows, he might not give the go-ahead for the series.'

The threat of withdrawal of publicity had the desired effect. Or rather one desired effect, in that the tallest boy gave Janine's address. Since it was the old one, the effect was also undersired.

And left Charles no further forward. He puzzled as to how he could continue his questioning about Janine and remain in character.

But he was saved by the intervention of the girl called Polly. 'No, that's no good. Mike said she had moved from there.'

'Any idea where she might have gone?'

They all shook their heads blankly.

'You mentioned a boy-friend. Maybe I could trace her through him.'

'None of us ever met him. She kept herself to herself. I think it must've been one of those very tight neurotic sort of relationships. Just the two of them in the flat, they never seemed to go out together.'

'Hmm. So you have no other possible contact for her?'

They all shook their heads again. Then the girl called Cookie said, 'I did once meet her mother. We were doing a date down in Croydon and had a free afternoon, so Janine suggested we went and had a cup of tea with her Mum.'

'Do you remember the address?'

'Yes, but I don't think she'd have gone there now. I got the impression they've had a row of some sort. I think it was about the boy-friend. Janine only once mentioned him to me. Said her mother didn't like him and, if it came to a choice between her mother and her man, it'd have to be the man.'

'She didn't say his name?'

'No.'

'Well, could you give me her mother's address? It might be a great help.'

'I don't think she'd be there if they didn't get on.'

'If she's broken off with the boy-friend, they might be friends again, she and her Mum.'

'Possible.' Cookie gave the address.

The tallest boy and the others were getting restless. 'Look, what is all this about Janine? I thought your article was meant to be about the group as it is now.'

'Yes, of course,' Bob Cherry assured them. 'Now tell me, what are your ambitions for the group over the next year?'

And, to allay their suspicions, Charles Paris condemned himself to another half-hour of corybantic aspirations.

●　　　●　　　●

He caught a bus from East Croydon Station. The investigation was beginning to get rather costly in travel. After paying off a few debts and building up his stock of Bell's whiskey, the fee for *The Alexander Harvey Show* was almost gone. Soon he'd have to get some more work. He'd call Maurice. It wouldn't get him a job, but it would make him feel he was doing something about it.

On the bus he thought about Janine Bentley. Strange how different people's views of her were. From almost everyone there came this picture of the quiet little girl, possibly rather repressed, living in a claustrophobic and private relationship with the unknown boy-friend. But how did that tally with Carla Pratt's description of the phone call to her, of this unbalanced 'spooky' character? Maybe Janine did have a split personality, her quiet manner hiding the seethings of a sick mind. That would make her motivation for murdering Billy Peaky much more comprehensible.

But Charles still had difficulty in relating this image of her with her appearance. He had only seen her on stage and in the publicity photographs (and had recent cause to remember how much the skills of make-up and hairdressing could falsify in such circumstances), but he had got an impression of a certain honesty in her, something that made a direct appeal to him. Not just a sexual attraction, but a warmth.

He also got the feeling that she was naturally beautiful. Though hairdressing had helped her long blonde hair to its bounce and sparkle, its luxurious abundance owed nothing to artifice. And her large blue eyes could not have been faked; they were God-given.

Yet he was looking for this girl as a murderer. All the evidence and logic pointed towards her guilt. Well, he was too old to be side-tracked by a pretty face.

The face, when he saw it, was not pretty.

He had rung the door chimes of the suburban semi where Mrs Bentley lived and been greeted by a voice from the other side of the door. A young voice, frightened, strained. 'What do you want?'

'Hello, I've come to see Mrs Bentley.'

'What about?'

'About her daughter, Janine.'

There was a pause for some reaction which he could not see. Then 'Mrs Bentley's out. What was it about exactly?'

Time for a risk, or at least a shock tactic. 'It's about Bill Peaky.'

This time the sound of the reaction was unmistakable. A little whimper of fear.

Another silence, then the door opened a crack. It was held inside with a chain. Charles could not see the face of the person who opened it.

'I don't recognise you.' There was still an undercurrent of fear, but a new note of fatalism flattened the tone.

'May I come in and talk?'

'I suppose it was only a matter of time before someone came,' the voice went on. 'I couldn't hope to hide here for ever.'

'May I come in?'

'Why not? You can't do any worse.' The door nearly closed as the chain was released, then opened.

And Charles saw the face.

It was Janine. He could recognise that. But it was a distorted Janine, almost a cartoon version. One cheek bulged sideways, pulling the face out of true. The memorable blue eyes glinted pinkly through the slits which were all the bruised eyelids left to open. The lips, puffy and cut, were slightly parted, stiff with pain, revealing the stump of a broken front tooth. Scratches carved straight roads over the irregular terrain of bruises.

But worst of all was the hair. The splendid opulence he remembered was gone. In some places it was bare to the scalp where it had been pulled out, in others straight edges showed where scissors had been enlisted to complete the destruction.

'Good God,' said Charles. 'Whatever happened to you?'

'There's no need to make it worse by pretending you don't know. Come inside. My mother will be back in half an hour, so you won't have long.'

Charles stepped inside the door and the girl closed it quickly. Then she stood back. He could not take his eyes off the ruin of her face.

'All right,' she said defiantly. 'Do your worst. I can't believe that anything can hurt me more than I've been hurt already.'

'What do you mean?'

'He said he would kill me. Is that why you've come? If it is, just make it quick.'

'What are you talking about? I haven't come to hurt you.'

'Don't play with me.'

'Listen, my name is Charles Paris. I was in Hunstanton when Bill Peaky died. I have reason to believe that his death was not as straight-forward as it may have appeared.'

'Then you haven't come to hurt me?'

Charles shook his head gently. Slowly the girl sagged as the fierce tension left her. Then the first wave of crying struck and her body shook as the emotion took over. Charles took her gently by the shoulders and led her into the sitting room.

After about five minutes the weeping subsided and she lay back in her chair, limp as a rag doll.

Charles felt an enormous weight of pity for the girl, but at the same time he knew that while she was weak and relaxed was a good time to tackle her about Peaky's death. 'Janine, I think someone tampered with the wiring of Bill Peaky's guitar and killed him deliberately.'

'Oh.' The inflated face looked at him vaguely. 'You mean he was murdered?'

Charles nodded.

'I never thought of that,' said the girl, still bemused. But then she seemed to see some logical consequence of the premise and became animated. 'No. He couldn't have been. You must be wrong.'

'I don't think so.' Charles didn't like bullying this poor ruined child, but, having started, he pressed on. Make the conclusion swift. 'I know quite a lot about you, Janine. I know you were having an affair with Bill Peaky and I know he broke it off the day he died. I also know that you were ill, or pretended to be ill, after that scene with him. I am suggesting that you took your revenge on him by changing the wiring on his amplifier lead and thus causing his death.'

The girl's expression had altered subtly. Now it looked as if a smile might be on the broken lips. Charles knew that his speech didn't have the rhetorical force he had hoped for and he added, rather feebly, 'Well, what do you say?'

'I've no idea what you're talking about.' Her surprise sounded genuine. 'I changed the wires on his amplifier? I don't know what an amplifier looks like and I can't even change a plug. I think you are giving me credit for technical abilities I just don't possess. Where am I supposed to have picked up all this electrical knowledge?'

'You learnt it from your guitarist boy-friend.'

'Who, Bill?'

'No, the one before. The one in the rock group.'

'I never had boy-friend in a rock group.'

He felt an enormous desire to believe her. She looked so vulnerable, poised gingerly on the armchair. But he knew he must not be swayed by sentiment. If the girl were really mentally ill, with homicidal tendencies, then he must take no risks.

'Listen, Janine, I've been through it all and the evidence against you is pretty convincing. Unless you can persuade me that you have an alibi for the time when the wiring was tampered with, then I think you had better start explaining a few things.'

'An alibi? What is this?'

'Let me refresh your memory about that afternoon. You danced with the rest of the group in the opening number of the show. Then you went to see Bill Peaky, who told you he didn't want to marry you. You had a row and then started to feel ill, either genuinely or for tactical reasons. As a result you didn't dance in the first half closer. A taxi was summoned to take you home, but I happen to know that it didn't arrive until the second half had started. That gave you plenty of time to fix the wiring. The old cable had been broken during Lennie Barber's act, but the new one was checked out at the beginning of the interval. So during the interval you crept backstage and changed the wiring.'

She leant back, all tension gone, exhausted. 'I think you must be mad. Or is this another of his elaborate games?'

'Whose?'

She looked piercingly at him for a moment. 'Never mind. So you are asking me for an alibi, are you? For the interval?'

'That's right.'

'As it happens, by coincidence, I have one.' The words were spoken without irony, just with infinite weariness. 'I sat with the theatre St John's Ambulance man right through the interval until my taxi arrived. His name's Harry. You can check with him. He's at the theatre for most performances. So many old bods go to the shows there, they need someone standing by with the oxygen mask.'

'Oh. I will check,' said Charles assertively. But even as he said it, he knew she was telling the truth. As so often in his detective career, he felt his paper house tumbling around him at the first seismic tremor of logic. There was a pause. Then he asked, 'Who beat you up?'

'It's not your business.'

'Was it your boy-friend?'

A tremble of her features betrayed the truth, but she repeated, 'I told you, it's none of your business.'

'And that's why you left the group so suddenly?'

'I could hardly turn up and dance sexily like this, could I? Assuming I could even move at the time, which I couldn't.' Her retort had a spark of character that suggested a warmer, livelier Janine who would be nice to know in happier times.

'And you thought your boy-friend had sent me to duff you up some more?'

'He said he'd kill me.' In her fear she forgot to deny that the beating-up was her boy-friend's work.

'When he found out about you and Peaky?'

'Yes. Oh, it was all such a mess. I had been with . . . him for two years and, I don't know, I suppose I thought all relationships were like that, all the anger and the silences, seeing no one else when we were together, all that. Then when I met Bill, he was nice to me, sort of jolly, didn't seem to take life seriously. And I thought it'd work.'

Poor kid. She was one of those girls doomed from the cradle only to get mixed up with men who were bastards. Gently Charles asked, 'How old are you, Janine?'

'Nineteen'. As she said it, she looked ten years younger, a child who had fallen over in the playground.

He felt a surge of anger. 'Good God. What kind of bastard does that to a girl?'

'You don't know him. He can be so kind, so gentle. He gets these black moods, though, and, well, he's got problems.'

'He certainly has.'

She looked at him, puzzled, then seemed suddenly to see an implication of his remark that worried her. 'Mr Paris, are you sure Bill was murdered?'

'Pretty sure.'

'I see. I think you'd better go.' She rose painfully to her feet.

Charles' reasoning was a few seconds behind her's, but now he understood what had caused her anxiety. 'I suppose,' he began casually, 'that your boy-friend's revenge might not have stopped with you.'

'I said I think you had better go.'

'He might see Peaky as equally guilty. Possibly more guilty.'

'My mother will be back soon.'

'And the kind of guy who would beat you up like that's not going to be too squeamish about murder.'

'I said go.'

'No. You tell me who he is. Who is your boy-friend?'

She stood before him, battered but defiant. 'I'll never tell you. And you won't find out from anyone else, because nobody knew.'

The second part of her assertion he doubted. If they had lived together for two years, even in the anonymous world of London flatland, someone must have seen them together.

But the first part he accepted. She wouldn't tell him. In spite of her injuries, she had an indomitable will. And Charles was feeling so depressed by the waste of her beauty that he could not bring himself to try to bully it out of her.

He left.


On the bus back to East Croydon Station, his mind worked slowly and logically through all she had said. And its conclusions were encouraging. Although Janine had not told him her boy-friend's name, she had narrowed down the possibilities dramatically.

Her sudden change of mood and subsequent shielding of his identity had shown that she believed in her boy-friend's guilt. Which meant that he must have had the opportunity to commit the crime. Which meant he must have been down at Hunstanton on the relevant afternoon. And must have been backstage during the interval.

It couldn't be anyone in the company. There was no way that he wouldn't have found out about the affair between Janine and Peaky when it started. Anyway her boy-friend was reported never to have gone on tour with her.

Charles thought back. Four people had gone backstage at the interval. Dickie Peck. Miffy Turtle. Paul Royce. And Walter Proud.

Dickie Peck Charles discounted as having nothing to do with the case. (For rather unprofessional reasons, as it happened. He had once suspected Peck in another case and been proved wrong.)

Miffy Turtle and Paul Royce, Charles knew little about. But anyway his thoughts leapt past them as a new suspicion took hold of him.

Walter Proud had divorced his wife a year before. How many middle-aged men before him had chucked up their settled life for a last fling with a young girl? Walter Proud used to be moody and was now drinking heavily. In a drunken fit he would be capable of acts of violence.

What was more, Walter Proud had started life as a sound technician. He understood the mysteries of electrics and wiring.

From every point of view, he seemed to be the likeliest person to have murdered Bill Peaky.

## Chapter VIII

COMIC: An agent's trying to sell one of his acts
to a night club owner. 'You gotta see this girl.
She's got an amazing body. Her vital statistics
are 75-23-36. And what an act!'
'What does she do,' asks the owner, 'dance?'
'No. She just crawls on to the stage and tries to
stand up.'

Fate seemed to read his thought and when Charles got
back to his Hereford Road home he found a note,
scrawled by a Swedish girl from one of the other bedsitters, that 'Moritz Skollen' had phoned and, when he
rang Maurice Skellern, he was given a message to contact Walter Proud at the television company which
made *The Alexander Harvey Show*. Fate seemed to be
setting up a confrontation.

After a bit of trouble with the switchboard, who
didn't appear to have heard of Walter Proud, Charles
got through. He found his prospective murderer in
buoyant mood.

'I've pulled it off, old boy.'

'What?'

'A pilot of a show with Lennie Barber. Nigel Frisch
saw the interview with Alex and he thinks we may be
on to a winner. May have just judged the nostalgia cycle
right. So it's all systems go.'

'When does it happen? The year after next?' asked

Charles, familiar with television scheduling.

'No, it's a real rush job. In the studio in six weeks.'

'Phew.'

'The studio date was reserved for a special with Bill Peaky.'

'What? The thing you were seeing him about?'

'Yes, yes.' Walter brushed the idea aside and pressed on. 'But it's really great news, isn't it? I mean, it won't just be recreating Barber and Pole routines, though there'll be a bit of that. Lots of new material, really make it a kind of sketch show, with variety acts, of course. Pop singer guesting, maybe, a few dancers.'

'These Foolish Things,' Charles threw in, to see if the name prompted any betraying reaction.

It didn't. 'Shouldn't think so. Should be one of the bigger names. Well, what do you say? Great, isn't it?'

'Yes, certainly,' said Charles with guarded enthusiasm. Guarded because, though it was possible that Walter was ringing to say that, after his initial success in the role of Wilkie Pole, he would play the part again in the new show, Charles had been in the business too long to make that assumption. It was just as likely that Walter was ringing to tell him, thank you very much, thought you were super, love, but I'm afraid the part's going to the Dagenham Girl Pipers.

Fortunately this uncertainty was settled by the producer's next words. 'Of course you must come back and do your Pole, but it won't just be the two of you. We're going to open it out quite a lot, bring in a few other younger character boys and girls for the sketches. I think it's going to be very big. Look, as I say, the pilot's in the studio in six weeks, so we'll want you available for filming from about the 3rd of next month. I checked availability with Maurice and he didn't seem to think there was a lot in the book, unless it was something you had set up and not told him about.'

'Well . . .' At such moments Charles was always tempted to play hard to get, mumble mysteriously about talk of a film, possibility of a telly series and so on.

Nobly he restrained himself. 'No, that should be fine.'

'OK. Well, I'll put the booking through and my casting director will be in touch with Maurice. Listen, as it's such a rush job, I want to get talking about it as soon as possible. Now Lennie Barber's doing his act at a club this week. Booking he got after *The Alexander Harvey Show*. The Leaky Bucket in Sutton, don't know if you know it?'

'No.'

'Well, I was thinking of going, sort of to see what kind of a night-club act he's doing these days, talk through some ideas for the show. Also getting a couple of writers along who I think could be the right combination for the show. Steve Clinton and Paul Royce, do you know them?'

'I've met Paul Royce. Never heard of Steve Clinton.'

'Dear oh dear, where do you hide yourself? Steve's one of the biggest names in the comedy field. Writes for Phil O'Neill, for a start. And he did that sit-com for Thames, the one set on a cross-Channel ferry, called *A Bit on Each Side*.'

'Sorry, I've never heard of it. And what's a sit-com? Is it one of those chairs with a chamber-pot incorporated?'

'No, you're having me on, Charles. Sit-com—situation comedy. Anyway, do you fancy joining us for the trip? Lennie's on about eleven, so it could be a late night. I'm meeting up with the boys and their agent, Virginia Moult, in the bar here at about nine, so's we can have a few drinks and then get a car down. Could be a good evening.' Beneath the big-time image, there was a lonely appeal in Walter's voice.

'Sounds interesting. I'd like to come.'

'Great. It'll continue your education. Don't you worry, Charles, we'll soon have you understanding how comedy works.'

After the conversation, Charles was conscious of the opposing pulls of his two careers, as an actor and as a detective. He knew that the mild elation he felt was because Walter had offered him a job, not because his supicions about the producer as a murderer were hardening into certainties. Oh well, time enough to check out his theories of Bill Peaky's death. The main thing was, it was work.

The Leaky Bucket in Sutton was one of those little clubs which closes and reopens every six months or so under a different name. Its existence was based on the fallacy that people in the London suburbs won't make the effort to go up to town and want a night spot on their doorstep. A relay of new owners and managers discovered for themselves the falsity of this premise, in their own time, with their own money.

In its recent incarnations it had been The Horseshoe, a drinking club, Kickers, a discotheque, The Closet, a gay club (much to the fury of the local residents), The Safety-Pin, a punk-rock club, and The 39 Steppes, a club with an emphasis on vodka and Russian cuisine. This last venture had only survived a fortnight, which was short even by the standards of the premises.

But now a new owner of unfailing (and unjustified) optimism had reopened it as a cabaret club, with a resident live group for dancing and 'The best of the world's entertainers' (to quote from the club's literature) for entertainment. The people of Sutton greeted the new incarnation with the same apathy they had lavished on its previous manifestations and the new owner started to lose money in exactly the same way as his predecessors.

However, it was a Friday night when Walter Proud and party entered the premises and there was a reasonably good turn-out. As they swam down into the smoky and red-lit interior, most of those present were dancing vigorously to the pounding of the live group which, to Charles' surprise, turned out to be none other than those stars of the Hunstanton bill, Mixed Bathing.

The intervening weeks had given them nothing more in the way of style, though their trade-mark, volume, was more noticeable in the confined space.

The club was not so full that a table could not be found for them and the club's new (and soon to be impoverished) owner, who had been tipped off about their coming by a phone-call from Walter, greeted them and presented a bottle of indifferent champagne 'with the compliments of the management'. At least Charles gathered from his fulsome face that that was what he was saying; the noise of the group made the words completely inaudible.

It also precluded the possibility of much conversation among the new arrivals and, to Charles' relief, even silenced Steve Clinton. It had become apparent in the television company bar and in the car on the way down that he was one of those writers who is a performer manqué and makes up for this by telling jokes all the time. Steve Clinton could be guaranteed to be the life and soul of any party, a characteristic which Charles found about as appealing as a slug in a salad.

Paul Royce, by contrast, was very quiet. All the ideas went on in his head and were only given life by being written down. This, Walter Proud had confided in Charles, was why he thought they were going to be *very big* writing together. All the great writing teams, he asserted, were made up of an extrovert and an introvert. Walter also had theories about the combination of experience and youth, which he thought would be ideal to produce the right material for Lennie Barber. Virginia Moult, the agent who represented both writers (Clinton for some years, Royce as of very recently), also thought it would make a good team and was confident that the coupling would pull up Paul Royce from beginner's rates to a much more reasonable level of script payment. In fact, she announced, she always tried to start new writers in tandem with more experienced ones because this confused the television companies' Copyright Departments in discussions of money.

Charles found Virginia Moult interesting. He looked at her as they sat silent amid the thundering music of the club. Short hair, had been all black, now streaked with grey. Prominent, determined nose. Hard set of mouth belied by unexpectedly full lips. Shortish, large bust, probably just turned forty. Wedding ring. Very tough, but not unfeminine. Interesting.

Walter Proud had entered the club with a self-important air and looked around as if he expected to be recognised all the time. He liked the big showbiz bit, television producer appearing in little-known venue, researching entertainment at grassroots level. The manager's obsequious gesture with the champagne coincided exactly with his self-image.

Walter's craning round was eventually rewarded by the sight of someone he knew. At a small table near the group's speakers sat Miffy Turtle, deep in conversation with an emaciated figure whom Charles recognised with some shock. It was Chox Morton from the Hunstanton inquest.

The initial reaction of amazement at this coincidence was tempered when Charles considered that, as the group's manager and roadie respectively, Miffy and Chox were quite likely to be seen at Mixed Bathing's venues. And also, when he thought about it, since Miffy also handled Lennie Barber's bookings, it made sense that here, as at Hunstanton, the comedian and the group should appear on the same bill. No doubt Miffy Turtle had arranged some sort of package deal with the club.

The agent caught Walter Proud's eye and waved vaguely. The producer sat back with satisfaction at having registered his identity and looked round for others to impress.

But the boppers of the Leaky Bucket manifested no interest in the media mogul; they were far too involved in their partners on the dance floor. This space was so small that, though most of Mixed Bathing's music was up-tempo, the only possible dance was a close-contact pelvic wiggle. The dancers had all been there drinking for some time and their only interests were carnal. Their

plans for the rest of the evening appeared to be to dance
a bit more and then get their partners as quickly as
possible on to beds, sofas or back seats of cars (according to domestic circumstances).

It was on to this schedule that Lennie Barber was imposed. Not ideal circumstances. Introducing cabaret
(particularly comedy) into an evening's entertainment is
a difficult skill to master, but a comedian starts at a
disadvantage if his appearance interferes with the
customers' eating, conversation or (in this case)
foreplay. There was an old threat that used to be used
by compères of nude girlie shows to rowdy audiences,
'If you don't keep quiet, I'll bring the comic back
on again' and it was with this kind of resentment that
Lennie Barber's appearance was greeted.

Mixed Bathing concluded another of their musical
demolition jobs and, while the room still shuddered in
the shock-waves, the manager came to the microphone.
After blowing into it and tapping it to see that it was
working, he made an announcement. Over the grum-
bling of the couples who had to prise themselves apart,
the noisy exit of the group and the vocal rush to the bar,
the words 'cabaret', 'great old comedian' and 'Barber'
could be heard by those who were trying hard. Without
further ceremony, Lennie Barber came to the microphone.

He was wearing a dark blue dinner jacket with satin
lapels and a light blue frilled shirt. A large navy velvet
butterfly had settled on his throat. The image seemed
wrong, an old mutton joint dressed as a Crown of
Lamb. It gave no impression of the sharpness of his wit;
he was just another gift-wrapped entertainer, with all
the individuality of a stereo music centre.

'Good evening, ladies and gentlemen,' he bawled over
the chaos. A diluted spotlight picked him out in the
prevailing red murk. 'I must say, before tonight I had
never been to Sutton, but I'd heard about it. And I still
came. Actually, as I came into the club tonight, I said to

the doorman, I hear that Sutton is the arsehole of the world. Oh, says the doorman, and you're just passing through?

'Actually, I got here a bit early, had some time to kill. Feeling a bit randy I was. Met this old girl in the street. I said, hey, darling, where's the night life of Sutton? She said, I am.

'Mind you, the tarts here are nothing. Best tarts I know are in Manchester. Up there they crossed a tart with a gorilla. Got one who swings from lamp-posts and does it for peanuts.

'Talking of tarts, bloke went to a prostitute and he said, look, I'm not going to pay you unless you guarantee that you're going to give me a dose of clap. It's all right, says the prostitute, you're bound to get it—why, though? Are you trying to get even with your wife? No, says the bloke, but if she catches it, the milkman will catch it, which means that Mrs Brown at Number 47 will catch it, which means that the grocer will catch it, which means that girl in the off licence will catch it, which means Fred Smith'll catch it—he's the one I'm trying to get even with. . . .'

It was rapidly becoming apparent that, like most comedians, Lennie Barber kept a special blue act for the clubs. It was also apparent to Charles that the style suited him as badly as the costume. The individuality was gone and Lennie Barber was reduced to a stereotype of a club comedian.

But he was getting through to the audience. A few had left for carnal purposes as soon as he came on and his first few lines were almost drowned in catcalls and conversation, but he persevered, slamming his jokes down with sledgehammer subtlety, cowing the audience into submission with the force of his personality. That certainly came through, even with the inappropriate image and unwholesome material. Charles felt again what he had in Hunstanton, not that he was watching the greatest act in the world, but that the man's potential was enormous. In the most uncongenial of circumstances, you had to watch him.

From being cowed, the audience began to be amused. The material remained unattractive, tales of sex and scatology, but it seemed to be what they wanted. Each punch line was greeted with the right shout of shocked laughter. More and more faces turned to the spotlit figure, sweaty faces with mouths slightly open in anticipation of the next crudity.

And, as he won the audience, Lennie Barber began to woo them, to force them to his rhythm rather than bending himself to theirs. He slowed down, stopped pile-driving his jokes, started to use silence and work with his face. Now that he had their attention, he let the audience see his full range of expression. His eyes popped lasciviously in the character of young men, fluttered with false sophistication for tarts, bleared rheumily as impotent dodderers and closed in obscene ecstasy for images of consummation.

But as his spell began to work, he started to dilute his material. Now that the audience was watching him, it no longer needed the hook of dirty words. His jokes became more whimsical, more attractive. Charles began to relax. He was in the presence of a master. Soon all the props of stereotype would be dropped and they would be watching the real Lennie Barber.

But the act never reached that point. In one of the pauses that the comedian was now daring to leave longer and longer, there was a harsh commotion from the bar. Voices were raised in anger. There was a sound of breaking glass.

Charles turned with the rest of the audience to see thrashing figures in the gloom. From the shimmer of their garments they seemed to be members of Mixed Bathing. Only two were actually fighting, while the rest of the group struggled to prise them apart.

There was a grunt, a curtailed scream and a guttural

sound. As the overhead lights were swtiched on with
sudden blinking intensity, Charles saw the silver-vested
vocalist/guitarist back away from the drummer, who
held a broken bottle. The vocalist turned to show the
waterfall of blood that was his face, before he toppled
forward on to the floor.

## Chapter IX

FEED: Do you talk to your wife while you are
    making love?
COMIC: Only if she telephones.

Mixed Bathing's vocalist was not seriously hurt. In the
sense that there was no damage to anything except his
looks. He would go round for the rest of his life marked
like a hockey ball and maybe he would have less success
with pop-crazed teenage girls, but he was not seriously
hurt.

The police had been called and, after taking brief
statements from some of those present, they left with
the drummer. The vocalist went off in an ambulance.
Apparently the antagonism between them had been of
long standing, brought to a head by an argument over a
girl.

Most of the club's clientèle had left by the time the
police arrived. Certainly there was no hope of recap-
turing the evening's atmosphere, either the mounting
eroticism of the dancing or the spell created by Lennie
Barber. Anyway, it was after twelve when the fight happened and the club closed at one.

But people lingered and the manager didn't take a lot
of persuading to keep the bar open for Walter Proud's
party, Miffy Turtle, Chox Morton and a couple of the
members of Mixed Bathing. Everyone needed a drink
after the shock.

'Trouble was,' said Mixed Bathing's rhythm guitarist,

'they didn't agree about the music neither. Nick always said we wanted really to get into punk in a big way and Phil thought we ought to appeal to a more teenybopper, bubblegum market.'

Charles didn't know which of the fighters was which, but he felt it only appropriate that Nick the punkophile must be the drummer with the broken bottle.

'Yeah,' Mixed Bathing's keyboard player agreed gloomily. 'Like from the start I've always thought we ought to have been into a funkier sound anyway. More kind of laid-back, less up-front, know what I mean?'

Disconcertingly, Charles found that this remark seemed to be addressed to him. 'Sort of,' he offered hopefully.

'Still, now Nick and Phil've split that's really screwed the whole scene. Been a heavy trip last few months, anyway. Guess we'll all just get back to our musical roots now.'

'How do you mean?' asked Charles, intrigued in spite of himself.

'Well, like I'm really into good old fifties R and B. Wiggy—' he indicated the rhythm guitarist, 'Country's really his scene. You know, I guess we'll get it together in our own ways, go back to basics, from the top, no hassles, know what I mean?'

This time Charles felt that to nod or agree that he did know what the keyboard player meant would be dishonest, so he said nothing.

'But you mean it's the end of the road for the group?' Chox Morton's voice was small and anxious. He sat nervously forward on his stool, impossibly thin, fingering his glass of Coke.

'Gotta be, hasn't it, Chox? I mean, I don't reckon we could have stuck together long anyway. The vibes were getting really heavy. But after this . . .'

'Yes, Mixed Bathing's finished.' Miffy Turtle spoke with authority and a kind of realistic gloom.

'No more Mixed Bathing. The boys will be taken down to the Baths with their costumes on Monday and the girls will be taken down on Tuesday. Which means the Gym Master will have his hands full.' Steve Clinton laughed immoderately at his innuendo. To give everyone else their due, they ignored him.

'But what about tomorrow night at the club?' the manager asked Miffy. 'I mean, the group's booked in to the end of the week.'

'Well, come on, use your loaf. They won't be here, will they? One of them'll be in bleeding hospital and the other will be in the bleeding nick. You'll have to make do with records for the kids to bop to.'

'Be a darned sight cheaper.' The manager spoke with venom festered by an old grievance.

'Look, if you want a decent group to come to a hole like this, you have to bloody pay for it. We ain't bloody amateurs.'

'You'll be in breach of contract if the group doesn't turn up tomorrow.'

'Stuff it, Mr DeMille. There's bugger all you can do about it.' Miffy spoke with impressive force and the manager was silenced.

'Hear about the Irish rapist who tied the girl's legs together?' asked Steve Clinton, incapable of leaving silence unfilled and equally incapable of filling it with anything but a joke.

Again company solidarity prevailed and nobody took any notice of him. Charles looked across at Paul Royce, who was gazing morosely into his Scotch. The young man seemed even less amused by Steve Clinton than the rest of them. Maybe it was the prospect of writing with this walking Bumper Fun Book that depressed him. Walter Proud may have had his theories about introverts and extroverts complementing each other, but Charles couldn't see it working out for long with such extremes of facetiousness and gloom.

As he looked across at Paul Royce, he caught Virginia Moult's eye. She was staring at him hard, appraisingly. He felt an uneasy excitement.

Walter Proud sat next to her. Charles shifted his gaze

to the producer. The gin was getting through and, as it relaxed the face, Charles could see the sagging contours of age and sadness.

Walter was determined to be jovial, to put across the showbiz image of indestructability, but brashness could not hide the fear, the fear of ageing and of dying, the fear that could drive a man into the apparently rejuvenating arms of a young girl and that could turn him to violence if she rejected him. Charles could identify uncomfortably closely with Walter. He had known the blindness of sexual anger, the jealousy of a younger man's irretrievable advantage. If he had been in love with Janine and if he had been aced out by a cocky young comedian, he would not like to have predicted how he might have behaved.

Lennie Barber emerged from the cupboard that served as dressing room, drink store, laundry room, lavatory and manager's office. He got a bottle of Scotch and a glass from the bar and joined the wide circle of drinkers. He poured a big tumblerful and downed it.

'Going all right tonight, Lennie. Before the fight,' Miffy Turtle observed.

Barber shrugged wryly. 'Audience was rubbish.'

'But you was getting them round, Lennine. Act coming together very nicely.'

'Very nicely,' Walter echoed, with the indulgence of the big impresario. 'All very promising. Of course, the IBA wouldn't wear any of that material on telly, but the life is there and that's what matters. No, when this telly show gets away, it's going to be very big, very big indeed.'

'As the actress said to the bishop.' Nobody reacted to Steve Clinton's reflex line.

'What telly show's this?' asked Miffy Turtle, unnaturally quiet.

'Got a pilot away for Lennie. And Charles here. Following the success on the old *Alexander Harvey Show*. Very exciting prospect, going to be very big.'

'How long've you known?'

'Only got the definite go-ahead today. Something . . . fell through, so the studio date was suddenly available. I rang Lennie and Charles. Of course, I should have rung you, Miffy, as Lennie's agent, but—'

'Too bloody right you should have rung me. Yes, I'm his agent and don't you forget it. I'm not going to fart around getting him bookings in smelly little holes like this and then miss out on the big ones.'

'No one was suggesting that, Miffy. I was going to ring you tomorrow.'

'Oh yes, it's always bleeding tomorrow, isn't it?'

'Miffy, don't be bloody daft.' Lennie Barber spoke with dignity and authority. 'No one was trying to keep you in the dark about anything.'

'And no one had better bloody try it. I'm not going to lose all my bloody artists just when they start to take off.'

'Course you're not, Miffy. Calm down. All right, it looks like you've lost one of your acts tonight, so I can see you're sore. But Mixed Bathing wouldn't have stuck together more than a couple of months anyway. You could see the split coming, couldn't you?'

'Oh, sure, Lennie, sure.' Miffy Turtle's anger had subsided. 'I was just thinking, you used to be with the big agents when it was all happening for you. If it's all happening over again, maybe the big boys will start sniffing again.'

'If they do, I'll tell them what they can sniff,' said Lennie Barber coarsely. 'That load of shits didn't come near me when I was down on my luck. I don't give a damn about them. Anyway, Miffy, this is only one television programme, not a big deal. It's—'

'It is a big deal,' objected Walter, offended.

'No, it'll probably come to nothing. Nothing to get excited about. Like they used to say to the would-be comics at auditions: It's OK, but don't give up your day-job.'

'Now don't play it down, Lennie,' Walter protested.

'This show's going to put you right back on the map.'

'Yeah, but whereabouts?'

Walter ignored the cynicism and started being a producer. 'Actually, I wanted to talk about a few details on the show. First thing we've got to do is to get a script together. Can't really talk about that now, but maybe we could fix up a meeting tomorrow—no, that's Saturday—Monday, to talk about what we're going to do. OK for you Lennie? Paul? Steve?'

'In the words of the abacus, you can count on me.' Steve Clinton guffawed alone at his wit.

'But more than that, we've got to think positive on this show. Think big. We've got to say, this show is going to be the biggest comedy sensation of the year and Lennie Barber is going to be the biggest star.' Walter Proud was beginning to enjoy the Hollywood backstage movie in which he had cast himself. 'So what it means is, Lennie, you've got to be seen around a bit. Right sort of places. I mean, for instance, next Wednesday there's this UEF Awards lunch. The television company's got a table and you've got to be seen there, Lennie. With Charles here.'

'What's UEF?' asked Charles.

'United Entertainments Federation. Big do, being televised. We'll meet a lot of important people there and get a chance to let them know the show's happening. Got to think PR, you know.'

Lennie Barber grimaced. 'Jesus, I can do without all that show-business schmaltz.'

'That's not the point. It's important.'

'I'll see you there, Walter,' said Miffy.

'Oh, I didn't know that was your scene. What'll you be doing there?'

'Picking up an award?' asked Steve Clinton. 'Best Supporting Rôle—won by Miffy Turtle's truss.'

'In fact, I will be there to pick up an award. Most Promising Newcomer.'

'Most Promising Newcomer? You?'

'No. Bill Peaky.'

• • •

The mention of the dead comedian's name caused a long silence, as the collective memory recalled the shock of his death. Charles suddenly realised how many of those present had been in Hunstanton for that terrible matinée. Everyone except the manager of the Leaky Bucket, Steve Clinton and Virginia Moult.

Surprisingly, it was Chox Morton who voiced their common thought. 'It was horrible, that. Tonight was horrible, too, but not like that. I still see it sometimes in my dreams.' He paused, his thin face trembling. 'I won't ever forget what I saw that day.'

Charles looked quickly round to see if any of his potential suspects gave anything away. Predictably (according to his latest theory of the murder) Walter Proud seemed the most flustered. 'Well, we don't want to dwell on that, do we? Terrible tragedy, of course, but in this business you've got to look to the future. Doesn't do to get maudlin.'

'Funny, though,' Chox Morton's voice went on. It was distant, musing. 'Funny that Bill should have been electrocuted after we had been discussing it so recently.'

'Discussing electrocution so recently?' asked Charles with what he hoped was the appearance of diffident enquiry.

'Yes. I forget how we got round to the subject, but one day in Hunstanton, between a matinée and an evening show, somebody asked me about it, how that kind of accident happens. Got me to explain it all. Surely you remember that?'

'Yes, I remember,' said Lennie Barber, unconcerned. 'In the Green Room, wasn't it?' After Lennie had admitted remembering the incident, Miffy Turtle grunted agreement. So, surprisingly, did Walter Proud. Catching Charles' quizzical eye, he said, 'Yes, I was down that day.'

'Funny,' observed Charles hoping again that he sounded nonchalant. 'So it was just the four of you talked about it?'

'No, one of the dancers was there too,' said Miffy. 'Kid called Janine.'

Damn. It was getting impossible to eliminate anyone from this enquiry. Except Paul Royce. He hadn't been there, so he wouldn't have heard Chox's advice on how to commit electrocution. Charles longed to ask who had first raised the question, but feared that he couldn't make that sound like idle interest. Maybe he could get Chox on his own at some point and ask.

The roadie continued speaking in the same abstracted way—'We went through it in some detail. How the wires would have to get changed round for it to happen. Didn't realise at the time, it all seemed quite funny. Not funny in retrospect, though. I don't think I'll ever forget what I saw that day.'

He mesmerised them into silence.

Needless to say, it was Steve Clinton who broke it. 'I dunno. Sounds like the annual meeting of the Trappists' Debating Society.'

For once people seemed to take notice of him, or at least his words had the effect of breaking the rather eerie mood Chox had created. 'Come along, gents, got to be closing soon,' said the manager.

'Yeah, I'd better go and get my gear together.' Chox disappeared behind the curtain that led to the boxroom and lavatory.

'Now anyone fancy coming back to my place in town for a quick nightcap?' asked Walter Proud heartily. But his forehead was glistening with sweat and Charles could see in his eye the glint of fear. Was it just the fear of being left on his own or was there more to it?

Charles waited to see how the others reacted to the offer before he answered. A little plan was forming in his head, a plan that had absolutely nothing to do with detective work. He had noticed that Virginia Moult had come in her own car.

He also noticed with satisfaction that she declined Walter's invitation. And, with growing satisfaction, that Miffy Turtle, Paul Royce and Steve Clinton accepted it. He looked at Lennie Barber, urging acceptance on him.

'I may come, Walter.' The comedian grimaced. 'Sorry, got a touch of the old gut. I'll be back in a min. Just got to go to the khazi.' He moved with some pain towards the lavatory.

Charles stood in front of Virginia Moult. 'Where the hell's Sutton?' he asked.

'What do you mean?'

'Well, which tube line's it on? Which rail line? Is it near an airport? How does one get from it to anything like a civilised part of London?'

'God, I wish I had your subtlety. Yes, all right. I'll give you a lift.'

'Thank you very much.'

'Where do you live?'

'Bayswaterish.'

'I live in Chiswick.'

'That sounds very nice.' Bless you, Arthur Bell and Sons for the silver tongue your whisky gives me. Why the hell can't I chat women up when I'm sober? 'I couldn't help noticing,' he continued while the mood was on him, 'that you seem to be wearing a wedding ring.'

'Funny that. Must be because I'm married.'

'Ah. That would explain it.'

'Yes. He's in Rome for a month.'

'Ah.'

'Car's parked just round the back of this place.'

'Great.' Then with a sudden access of detective conscience, 'Must just go and have a quick word with someone. See you out there.'

'Don't be long. It's late.'

As Charles pushed through the curtain to the back of the club, he met Lennie Barber emerging. 'Better?'

'Yeah. Bloody guts. Still, can't complain. My usual trouble's constipation, so I suppose this is a step in the right direction. Wish it was only a step rather than a bloody trot, though.'

'You going back to Walter's?'

'Yes. Never sleep too good straight after the act.'

How considerately everyone was playing into his hands, Charles thought.

Chox Morton was packing up a small bag of electrical equipment. He jumped like a rabbit when Charles approached. 'What do you want?'

'Chox, you know you were talking about Hunstanton . . .'

'What about it?'

'Saying how you discussed electrocution from guitar amplifiers.'

'So what?'

'Can you remember who actually raised the subject? Who first asked about electrocution?'

'Here, what is this?' Chox moved suddenly to get past, but Charles reached out quickly and grabbed the boy's wrist.

The reaction was incredibly fast. Chox's free hand shot out and karate-chopped at Charles forearm, numbing it and freeing him.

The roadie nursed his wrist. His thin face was tight with emotion. The sunken eyes glared feverishly. 'Don't you ever touch me like that.'

'What do you mean? I just wanted to ask you a question.'

This seemed to relax him. 'Yes, Yes, of course. I'm sorry. I . . . I over-reacted. I . . .' The boy fought for coherence. 'I've had some trouble in the past . . . with homos, know what I mean? Sorry, I just don't like people touching me.'

'OK. Sorry to grab you like that.'

'Forget it.' The roadie turned to leave.

'All I want you to tell me is, who raised the subject of people being killed by electrocution from guitar amplifiers?'

Chox looked back at Charles, a small smile twisting his thin lips. 'I can't remember,' he said, and left.

•    •    •

Virginia Moult's cottage in Chiswick was neat and Victorian, like a set for one of those turn of the century television series that sell so well aboard. The bedroom was the largest room, though that didn't say much. By the time the bed had been fitted in, there wasn't a lot of space for anything else. Which meant there was little point in standing around. Charles flopped on to the bed.

Virginia moved to the pile of wafer-thin stereo equipment, stacked like filing trays on a walnut table. 'Do you like Music While You Work?'

'If it's good enough for the British Forces Network in Germany, it's good enough for me,' replied Charles, remembering the regular announcement on the famous radio programme.

Virginia slammed in a cassette and started to strip off. There were speakers either side of the headboard and the stereo was so good that Elton John was virtually in bed with them.

Virginia lay beside him, naked except for a silver whistle charm on a chain round her neck. That, with her large breasts and tightly prominent bottom, made her look like a gym mistress. And somehow Charles felt he was going to be put through his circuit training.

He reached over to her shoulder and crushed the duly satisfying breasts against his chest.

'Hey, there's no hurry,' she said. 'Weekend. You are hungry.'

'Eat when I can.'

'I, on the other hand, have regular meals.'

'Come on, you said your husband was in Rome for a month.'

'Yes, but he only left this morning.'

'Ah. What do you do it for?'

'Other men? Fatuous question.'

'Just fun, you mean?'

'That and . . . He's meeting his mistress in Rome.'

'Oh.'

'He's a film producer. She's in the movie. That's part

of the reason. Also I suppose there's time passing.'

'Cram as much experience in while you can?'

'Guess so. Dear God, you're a fat lot of good. When I want to go to bed with a *memento mori*, I'll look for a skeleton. Tonight what I had in mind was a real, live man.'

'Of course. Apologies for the maudlin turn of the conversation. Let's start again.' A pause. 'Nice music.'

'Yes, nice music. From my brand new stereo set-up. Very superior. And tax-deductible. Bought on the advice of one of my writers.'

'I didn't know writers were stereo buffs.'

'This one is. Very deeply into it. Actually, I think he's rather contemptuous of the stuff he recommended for me. He builds his own equipment. That's what the real experts do. Oh yes, what he doesn't know about plugs and transistors and amplifiers and leads isn't worth knowing. I went round to his flat once—only once, he didn't like people visiting, but I was curious—and, God, the great mound of hi-fi gear he'd got. Don't know how his girl-friend put up with it—except she wasn't around much. Off touring. Dancer or something.'

During this long, musing speech, Charles had found himself listening with mounting excitement. He could hardly find his voice to ask, 'Which one of your writers are you talking about?'

He knew the answer before she spoke. 'Paul Royce.'

'You say his girl-friend was a dancer.'

'Yes, with one of these pop modern lots. Not that I met her. He never brought her anywhere. I think they've broken up now, anyway.'

'Did he ever mention her name?'

Again Virginia didn't have to say 'Janine' before Charles' thoughts started on a Cresta Run of their own.

'Charles, I seem to be losing your interest again.'

'I'm sorry. I was miles away.' With a great effort of will he brought his mind to bear on the matters in hand. And very soon his concentration was rewarded.

## Chapter X

'Gerald, it must have been him. It all fits. He had the motive—the fact that Peaky was screwing his girl. He certainly had the violent temperament. Having seen what he did to Janine, I can vouch for that. He had the opportunity—he went backstage during the interval that day in Hunstanton. And, most important, he had the technical knowledge to commit the crime.'

'Who did you say you found this out from, Charles?' The solicitor's voice down the phone was tinged with suspicion.

'His agent, Virginia Moult.'

'Something in your voice tells me you have been tom-catting again. I don't know how you keep it up, Charles.'

'Nor do I, Gerald.' Charles picked up the innuendo with feeling. His body still ached from his protracted gym lesson.

'Don't be crude, Charles.'

'Sorry. It comes of mixing with all these comedians.'

'I think you should get back to Frances. Really organise yourself.'

'Hmm. I must ring her.'

'Anyway, what are you going to do about Royce?'

'I'll have to talk to him, confront him. There's no way I'm going to get any proof in this case, unless there's a missing eyewitness who's yet to come forward.'

'What about Janine?'

'What do you mean?'

'Suppose she saw Royce fiddling with the wires. And he beat her up to make her keep her mouth shut.'

'It's a possibility. She said she was with the theatre St John's Ambulance man during the interval.'

'Have you checked that?'

'No.'

'Well, it would be an easy lie so that she could claim ignorance of what lover boy did.'

'With lovers like that, that poor girl doesn't need enemies.'

Gerald's idea was a good one. The speed with which Janine had covered up her boy-friend's identity when Charles questioned her suggested that she at least thought him capable of murder. If she had actually seen him setting up the crime, her behaviour made even more sense.

'You don't fancy doing that, do you, Gerald?'

'Doing what?'

'Checking the alibi. When you say you're a solicitor, people'll tell you anything.'

'Then why don't you get on the phone and say you're a solicitor. It wouldn't be the first time. Come on, aren't you supposed to be a master of disguise?'

'My confidence in my abilities in that direction has been rudely shaken recently.'

'Oh, all right. I'll have a go.' Gerald was in fact glad of any crumbs of investigation which fell off the detective's table. Pursuing the image for a moment, Charles reckoned he was currently proving to be a rather messy eater.

'Meanwhile, I'll have a word with Royce.'

'I suppose you are likely to see him once you start rehearsal for this Lennie Barber pilot.'

'Think I'll see him before that. He's up for some script-writing award at this UEF lunch.'

'And you're going to be there?'

'Yes.'

'Doesn't sound your end of show business.'

'No, it isn't. Some mad idea of Walter Proud's. Get me and Lennie Barber seen about together. He reckons this'll ensure that the telly show is *very big*.'

'Not such a mad idea, actually, Charles. Subliminal effect. You know the award show's being televised, don't you?'

'Yes.'

'Well, don't wave at the camera, Charles. It's very unprofessional.'

Gerald was right. It wasn't Charles' end of show business. As he sat in the tartan ballroom of the Nelson Hotel, a new egg-box development in Park Lane, he began to realise just how far from his end of show business it was.

For a start, there was wearing a suit, a penance which Charles avoided whenever possible. And in this fathering of glittering trendies, he was awkwardly aware of the age of his suit, which was due for a come-back when the nostalgia boom reached 1962.

Then there was the company. Charles felt he had had rather a lot of sitting drinking too much with Walter Proud recently. To make things even more awkward, there seemed to be an atmosphere between Walter and the television company executives who occupied the rest of the table. Nigel Frisch was pointedly ignoring the producer, lavishing his attention on an actor and actress who had been nominated for awards for their parts in a soap opera about Edwardian vets. Charles wondered how Walter had managed to get the tickets for the event, since his presence seemed so much resented.

Lennie Barber, who might have cheered up the proceedings, was morose. He brooded darkly on his digestion. When they sat down, he drew Charles towards him and said, 'You know, what I always try to do is, every morning before I go out, have a good long sit on the lavatory, just wait till something happens, just wait, you know, before I leave the house. Doesn't always work.'

If that was going to be the standard of the comedian's repartee right through the meal, Charles could do without it.

The only person he did want to see was Paul Royce, but because he was up for a radio award, the writer was over on the BBC table. So there was no chance of making contact until the whole grisly affair was over.

The artificiality of the occasion depressed Charles. Nobody was there for anything but self-advertisement and yet all felt obliged to lavish greetings and insincere compliments on each other. Even the mild excitement of finding out who had actually won the awards (small gold-plated sculptures of escaped chair-springs) was defused by the fact that everyone present seemed to know the winners in advance. And those who didn't could work it out from the seating plan; the winners were placed at the ends of the tables nearest the stage, so that they could rise in simulated consternation and not be lost by the cameras.

The food was in keeping with the artificiality of the occasion. The Nelson specialised in what is euphemistically known as 'international cuisine'. The soup looked like soup, the meat was meat-shape and the vegetables were vegetable-shape; in fact it had all the qualities of real food except taste.

The televising didn't start until the actual handing-out of awards began, so there was a certain amount of moving about during the meal. At one point Dickie Peck, with his trade-mark of drooping cigar ash, came over to Charles' table. Walter Proud's vigorous wave was rewarded by a vague nod before the agent turned to Nigel Frisch. 'How's it going, Nigel? Want to talk to you about this new series idea for Christopher Milton.'

'Lovely. Right with you. Let's make it lunch at Wheeler's. Can you do tomorrow?'

'No. Friday any good?'

Frisch shook his head. 'Have to be next week.
Tuesday?'

The agreement was reached. 'By the way, Nigel.
Who's getting the Most Promising?'

'Bill Peaky. Posthumous.'

'Of course. I'd forgotten. Hmm. Funny, he was going
to join my stable.'

'Really?'

'Yes. I saw him the afternoon he died and we agreed
it. Hunstanton, of all places. There was a wasted trip.'
Dickie Peck seemed unaware of the fact that three other
people at the table had also been in Hunstanton on that
occasion. 'I suppose his widow picks the thing up. Oh
yes, there she is.'

Charles looked in the direction Dickie Peck indicated
and saw Carla at the end of one of the tables near the
stage. Deep in conversation with Miffy Turtle. She wore
a beautifully-cut black dress and Miffy's instinctive
flashiness was subdued into a charcoal grey suit. They
made an attractive couple. Charles couldn't help
visualising other circumstances, in which Bill Peaky
collected his own award. For Carla's sake, he had an
obligation to find out who had killed her husband.

The increase in the number of worried-looking men
with head-phones and the lumbering approach of
cameras and lights indicated that the televised part of
the proceedings was about to start. Rather than missing
Paul Royce in the confusion of everyone's departure,
Charles hurried across to the BBC table. 'Paul, I wonder, could we have a quick word after the ceremony.
Something I want to ask you about.'

The morose young writer looked at him cynically.
'You might at least wait till you get the script before you
start rewriting it.'

'No, it's nothing to do with the show. Something
else.'

Paul Royce looked at him sharply. ''OK I'll hang
about.'

'We could have a drink or something.'

'Sure,' said Royce and Charles could feel the boy's
eyes following him back to his seat.

The awards ceremony was compèred by a well-loved
television personality, who earned enormous amounts
of money by asking grown-up people childish questions
and rewarding them with consumer durables in the
shape of freezers, music centres, kitchen units and cars.
The show on which he regularly performed this repellent
function was called *The Take-Away Show*, so he opened
the awards ceremony with a coy little joke including his
catch-phrase, 'Take it away!' This was greeted by a
round of applause and sycophantic laughter. The well-
loved television personality then said how very very
honoured he was to be asked to compère the show and
how very very delighted he was to see so many popular
and well-loved faces in the audience. At this point the
cameras scanned round and picked out one or two of
the faces which were more popular and better-loved
than the others. To Charles' embarrassment he saw a
camera with a red light on trained on him and Lennie
Barber. Well, it was no doubt trained on Lennie Barber,
but the angle was such that Charles was bound to figure
in the shot. He gave a watery smile, hoping that he
looked popular and well-loved.

After a few merry quips about some of the senior
executives of the television companies and the com-
mittee members of the UEF (a bunch of accountants
and actuaries tickled pink at mixing with the world of
show biz), the well-loved television personality started
to introduce the actual awards.

The ceremony followed the mindless pattern that was
fixed for such occasions in Jurassic times and which has
not changed since:

The well-loved television personality would introduce
another well-loved television personality who had
nothing to do with the awards; this new well-loved
television personality would then deliver a couple of

scripted jokes and receive an envelope in which were the
names of the three nominations for the award; he would
then read out these names in reverse order; whereupon a
third well-loved television personality, the one who had
won the award, would rise from his convenient seat in
well-feigned amazement and go forward to receive his
chair-spring. If he were a man, he would then make a
very boring little speech thanking all of the production
team who had made it possible; if she were a woman,
she would start to make a boring little speech thanking
all of the production team who had made it possible,
but after a few words dissolve in tears. At this point the
audience would go 'Aah'. It was a time-honoured, un-
changing ritual and, incidentally, a very cheap way of
making a television programme.

The ideal at these ceremonies is to present an award to
a figure so old and so legendary in the business that
everyone thought he was dead (and, indeed, ideally, he
should die very soon after the ceremony). But when this
perfect climax cannot be achieved, a post-humous
award to a very young performer is a good second best.

So, though those present were constantly reminded of
the very wonderful and very heart-warming nature of
the occasion, the pinnacle of schmaltz was achieved
with the announcement of the award for the Most
Promising Newcomer.

Carla's approach to the stage was suitably affecting.
So was her little speech. After the trained voices of the
other winners, her thin Cockney sounded almost sin-
cere. And she didn't let the audience's expectations
down; there were real tears on her cheeks. Charles still
found it artificial, not because he did not believe in
Carla's feelings, but because the whole set-up seemed an
insult to genuine emotion.

To pile on the bad taste, after Carla's broken speech a
clip of Bill Peaky in performance was then shown on the
large screen at the back of the stage. Charles watched
with interest. The last time he had seen the comedian's
act had been in a sadly abbreviated version.

It took him about a minute to come to the conclusion that Bill Peaky had not actually been very good. There was a freshness of attack in the performance and some clever business with the guitar, but otherwise it was run-of-the-mill stuff. The well-loved television personality's mixed metaphor about 'one of the brightest flames that the entertainment firmament has seen this century so sadly extinguished so soon' (Good God, who wrote his stuff?) was just another example of showbiz hyperbole.

Having formed his own opinion of the late comedian's merits, Charles looked round to see what effect the clip was having on the potential murder suspects. Walter Proud was gazing at the screen with the proper maudlin awe. Lennie Barber, bored and slightly irritated, was modelling the inside of his bread roll into a dachshund. Miffy Turtle, helping Carla back to her seat in the subdued lighting, was not looking at the screen.

But on Paul Royce the effect was profound. The boy sat forward rigid in his seat. His face was set in a hard line of hatred.

When the last award had caused its studied surprise and the last drop of sentiment had been wrung from the occasion and the television recording had been cleared (presumably if there had turned out to be anything wrong with it, the whole process would have to be repeated and everyone be surprised all over again), the crowd of very wonderful people started to disperse. Charles hurried across to the BBC table, fearful of losing his quarry. But on his way he almost bumped into Carla Pratt. She was standing forlorn; Miffy Turtle was a little way away, talking to some prosperous-looking old men with cigars.

She reacted with some shock when she saw Charles. 'Mr Paris. I didn't expect to see you here.'

'I didn't expect to be here.'

She looked round quickly to see that no one was listening and then asked in a soft, urgent voice, 'Have

you got any further on . . . you know, what we talked
about?'

'I think so, yes.'

'Have you found Janine? Have you put the police on
to her?'

Oh yes, of course. When he had spoken to Carla, it
had seemed certain that Janine was the guilty party. His
mind had been through so many suspicions since then,
that it seemed a long time ago. 'Yes, I found her. But
no, I'm fairly certain she didn't kill your husband.'

'You mean, it was an accident after all?'

Charles shook his head. 'No, the further I get into the
case, the more convinced I become that he was murdered.'

'So you mean you suspect someone else?'

'Yes.'

'Who?'

'I can't really tell you yet. Quite soon, I hope.'

'You must tell me as soon as you have anything
definite. Ring me at any time of the day or night, please.
You must. I really want to know what happened. Let me
know even before you get in touch with the police.'

There was no questioning the sincerity of her emotion
now. She was deeply upset. Charles felt quite guilty for
suspecting her before. Obviously the emotion of the occasion and the sight of her husband on screen had
churned her up considerably.

'I'll let you know,' he said soothingly. 'I promise.'

Carla turned her head quickly to see Miffy Turtle approaching. With a look of complicity to Charles, she
moved off with her late husband's manager.

He took Paul Royce to the Montrose, a little drinking
club round the back of the Haymarket, which was one
of his regular haunts. The boy seemed subdued, almost
resigned. He hadn't asked Charles what it was all about,
just followed along unquestioning.

They both drank large Scotches. Charles decided to
leap in with both feet. 'Paul, I've seen Janine.'

The name prompted only a slight reaction. Paul Royce seemed to be dulled by depression. 'So?'

'I know about you and her. I know that you were living together.'

'So? What are you doing—taking on the rôle of my Moral Tutor. There's no law against people living together.'

'No, but there are laws against beating people up.'

This didn't produce the shock reaction Charles had hoped for; just a sardonic smile. 'Listen, Charles, I don't know what your game is, but why don't you mind your own bloody business? You know nothing about my relationship with Janine and, if I did beat her up, you can rest assured that I had a damned good reason for doing so.'

'You mean her affair with Bill Peaky?'

This did shake the writer, but he recovered himself quickly. 'My, you know everything, don't you?'

'I know quite a lot, Paul. I know, for example, that Bill Peaky was electrocuted.'

'Yes. That's my idea of poetic justice.' Royce spoke with enthusiasm. 'That's what he deserved, the little sod. Not only did he have the nerve to reject some bloody good material I sent him, he also seduced Janine. Electrocution was too good for him.'

'You hated him?' Charles asked gently.

'You bet I hated him.'

Charles paused, planning how he was going to play the scene. 'Paul, there's something else I know too.'

'What?'

'That Billy Peaky didn't die by accident.'

'You mean that somebody . . . did away with him?'

'Exactly that. Somebody deliberately switched the wires in the cable to his amplifier, so that his guitar would become live. Somebody who hated him very much did that. And he did it during the interval of the show that afternoon.'

Paul Royce looked at Charles blankly. It was impossible to gauge what thoughts lived behind the writer's sleepy, depressive's eyes. Charles pressed home his advantage. 'I also know, Paul, that you are a hi-fi expert and would have had no difficulty in altering the wiring. I know you went backstage at the interval that day in Hunstanton. You've just told me how much you hated Peaky and, having seen what you did to Janine, I don't find it difficult to believe that you are capable of killing.'

There was a long silence before Paul Royce spoke. When he did, his voice was soft, almost amused. 'I see. So that's it. Well, I never did. And I mean that literally too. I never did. Sure, I hated Peaky. I was delighted that he was killed. I don't make any pretence about that. But no, I didn't kill him.' He mused for a moment. 'Funny, it never occurred to me that he might have been murdered. I thought his death was just serendipity, divine intervention to show that, in spite of the bad press He tends to get these days, God still has a sense of justice.

'However . . . since you think I murdered him, I had better produce my alibi, had I not? Yes, I went back-stage that afternoon in Hunstanton. I went backstage with Walter Proud, Dickie Peck and Miffy Turtle—dear God, sounds like the Seven Dwarfs. We got to Bill Peaky's dressing room and he wasn't there. Miffy and Walter went off to find him. I stayed in the dressing room with Dickie Peck, failing to find any subject in which we were both interested, in fact failing to find any conversation at all. I wasn't out of his sight, though, for the whole interval. You can check, if you like.'

'I will,' asserted Charles vehemently, but the vehemence was reaction against the toppling of yet another of his houses of cards. Paul Royce was an un-pleasant young man, he had treated Janine Bentley un-forgiveably, but he had not killed Bill Peaky.

A new thought suddenly came rushing into the vacuum. 'Tell me, when Peaky came into the dressing room, were Walter and Miffy with him?'

'No. Walter came back a few minutes later. He had been to the lavatory. Miffy didn't come back. I got the impression he was rather . . . pardon the pun . . . miffed at the presence of Dickie Peck.'

'I see. Yes, he was Peaky's manager and just when his client was about to hit the big time . . .'

'The big boys started to move in.' Paul Royce finished the sentence for him. He rose to his feet and spoke with heavy sarcasm. 'Well, this has been delightful. Next time you want to accuse me of murder, don't hesitate to get in touch. I'm afraid I must be going now. If I get into the habit of drinking whisky all afternoon, I'm going to end up as a debauched middle-aged incompetent.'

The was no mistaking the barb in that parting shot, but Charles' mind was too full to take much notice of the unpleasant young man's departure. Unfortunately, it wasn't constructively full, just clogged with conflicting theories and unformed suspicions. Out of the confusion only one image was clear—Carla's face, wracked with genuine pain. *Do let me know.*

Maybe another talk to the victim's widow would clear his mind about the murder.

## Chapter XI

COMIC: I dreamt about your wife last night.
FEED: Did you?
COMIC: No, she wouldn't let me.

When he got back to Hereford Road Charles rang Carla's number. It was engaged. He tried again ten minutes later. With the same result. He kept trying at ten minute intervals for over an hour. Either she was having a very long phone call or something was wrong.

He dialled the operator and asked for the line to be checked. They rang him back and said that the phone was not in use, but appeared to have been left off the hook.

Charles started to feel a little quickening of anxiety. He had seen too much of violence and its effects over the last few days. He decided to go out to Chigwell to check that all was well.

It was still a hell of a long way and the evening tubes and buses were interminably slow. As Charles joggled about in them, he tried to focus his mind on his suspicions. But names and details tangled infuriatingly like a board game, little hopeful ladders of logic counteracted by long snakes of conflicting evidence. His only constant impression was one of slight dread.

It was after nine o'clock when he reached the wrought-iron gates of the Peaky's bungalow. The moon had taken the night off and it was dark. All the curtains at the front of the house were drawn. The distant hum of traffic on a main road served only to accentuate the local silence.

He lifted the metal latch gently and opened the gate with care. Instinctively he trod on tiptoe and left the gate ajar to avoid the slight clang of closing it. He glided up the concrete path to the front door.

There was no light showing through the wrought-iron-framed window in the door. The house seemed locked up in its own silence; nothing offered hope of any life within.

Still, it was worth ringing the doorbell to be sure. But as his finger moved towards the button, he checked it. No, not yet.

He moved back gently from the front door and looked at the bungalow. Yes, there was a slight blur of light on the lawn to the left-hand side. Still slowly, with his weight poised on the balls of his feet, he moved round to its source.

The shaft of light came from a thin triangle at the bottom of imperfectly closed curtains. Breathing shallowly, Charles moved towards the window. He peered through.

He was looking into what must have been Bill and Carla's bedroom. It was dominated by an enormous circular bed. But it was what he saw on the bed that snatched his breath away in shock.

Two naked bodies writhed in the paroxysms of love. Carla's face was turned to the window, the eyes closed, the mouth open, gasping with pleasure. The man's face was hidden, buried in her shoulder.

Their bodies arched and snapped together as they climaxed. Then they subsided, panting. After the moment the man drew away from her. Charles saw the chunky gold identity bracelet on the wrist and when the mystery lover swung his legs round to sit on the bed, he could see the man's face clearly.

It was Miffy Turtle.

# Chapter XII

COMIC: Two girls talking—one says to the other, 'Are you going out with your boy-friend to-night or are you going to sit in and watch television?'

'Doesn't make a lot of odds, really,' says her friend. 'Either way I get a lot of interference.'

The unfamiliar experience of being in work meant that Charles could not immediately pursue his detective investigations, but it gave him time to collect his ideas.

He had decided against confronting the post-coital couple in Chigwell until he had a clearer idea of what to confront them with. But what he had seen turned on its head everything he had hitherto thought about the case.

As he walked from Anerly Station to the RNVR Drill Hall, Wilberforce Street, where the rehearsals for *The New Barber and Pole Show* were being held, he tried to piece together a new version of Bill Peaky's murder.

The important change from all the previous versions was that Miffy Turtle was now cast in the rôle of villain. With that alteration to the Dramatis Personae, a lot of previously indigestible details were liquidised and made palatable.

Charles started from the assumption that the affair between Miffy and Carla had been going on for some time. It was possible that the agent had just been cashing in on the widow's loneliness the previous

evening, but the logic was stronger for a relationship
which had started while Peaky was alive. And Charles
could now define an impression he had received at the
awards ceremony, of a relaxed closeness between the
couple. An affair of long-standing also gave Miffy an
excellent motive for wanting Peaky out of the way.

Nor was that the only reason for him to kill his client.
There was something else that Charles should have
deduced in Hunstanton, but had only realised when
Dickie Peck mentioned it at the awards lunch. The London agent's sole purpose in going to Hunstanton was
to sign up the rising comedy star and, by doing that,
he was going to ace out the manager who had struggled
up with his client from obscurity. Miffy's outburst to
Lennie Barber in the Leaky Bucket Club showed how
sensitive he was to the dangers of losing his artistes just
at the point when they began to make real money. If Bill
Peaky was as unpleasant and self-centered as everyone
suggested, he would have had no qualms about dump-
ing his old friend and agent. That, together with the in-
convenience of Carla's having a husband around, might
well push a wide boy like Miffy into crime.

The new theory also explained the inconsistencies in
Carla's behaviour. It had been strange that, when
nobody else had a good word to say for her husband,
she had painted a picture of a perfect marriage, while
admitting her husband's frequent infidelities. Charles
had yet to meet the wife who, whatever her protesta-
tions, was genuinely complaisant about her husband's
affairs.

And now he understood Carla's strange story about
Janine Bentley. Having met the dancer, albeit at a time
of great physical and emotional pressure, Charles had
been struck by her essential level-headedness. Though
this could have been one of the many smokescreens of
schizophrenia, he preferred to accept his own
assessment of her character than the unbalanced one
presented by Carla. Anyway, that had been too quick,
too glib. The widow knew he was coming full of

suspicions, so she had hastily provided him with a convenient focus for them.

Such behaviour made very good sense if Carla was protecting her lover. If she knew Miffy had killed Peaky, or even came to suspect him when Charles first mentioned the idea of murder, then it was in her interests not only to provide the name of a potential murderer, but also to present the image of a desolated widow, whose life had been ruined by the premature loss of a beloved husband. Given the facts of such and idyllic marriage cruelly cut off, it would never occur to Charles that Carla had anything to gain from Bill Peaky's death.

She had thought quickly that afternoon. Full marks to her. She had thrown him off the scent very effectively. But the strain of thinking on her feet had affected her performance of bereavement and it was that which had made Charles suspicious of her sincerity.

Yes, if Miffy had killed Peaky, everything made sense. Even as he thought it, another piece clicked into place. Miffy, on the scene at Hunstanton for much of the run of *Sun 'n' Funtime*, was much better placed than any of the other suspects to check out the theatre's electrical system and plan the crime.

New confirmatory thoughts kept sparking in Charles' mind. At last he was really on to something. He would have to go and talk to Miffy Turtle.

The readthrough in the RNVR Drill Hall was the first time that Charles had met the director of *The New Barber and Pole Show*, Wayland Ogilvie. Walter Proud had spoken much of the young man, commending his own original thinking in bringing an established drama director into the less gracious arena of Light Entertainment, and Lennie Barber had mentioned meeting the director over a preliminary script conference. But none of this had prepared Charles for the parrot-faced aesthete with gold wire-rimmed glasses and quilted Chinese jacket to whom Walter Proud introduced him. 'Looking forward to a long and happy association,' said the producer jovially.

'Hope so.' Charles smiled a stupid smile.

Wayland Ogilvie looked at him intensely for a moment. Then he spoke. 'Scorpio. I'm quite compatible with Scorpios.'

Charles' reactions were twofold. First, he thought astrology was an affection. And second, he was impressed in spite of himself that the director had got his sign right.

Also present at the readthrough were Lennie Barber, the two writers Paul Royce and Steve Clinton, a few hardened comedy support actors who had been cast in some of the sketches, Wayland Ogilvie's PA (a dauntingly attractive girl called Theresa), a Trainee PA, a Stage Manager, an Assistant Stage Manager and a Chief Petty Officer in full uniform. This last turned out to be an official of the RNVR, who gave a short talk on things that could not be done in the Drill Hall. After his departure, the Stage Manager was berated for having allowed him to appear in the first place.

They all sat round a formica-topped table at one end of the hall. The rest of the space was marked out with lines of different coloured tapes and upright posts on wooden stands. These were the entrances and the whole surrealist forest represented the set (later in the day to be explained by the designer, who appeared in a beige corduroy boiler-suit).

Walter Proud welcomed everyone, saying how marvellous they all were and how *very big* the show was going to be and how he, as producer, would be keeping a very low profile and putting everything in the capable hands of Wayland Ogilvie and, once again, how, with a combination of the best artistes and the best writers in the profession, the show could not fail to be *very big*.

During this speech Charles observed Lennie Barber. The old comedian's face bore a smile of unambiguous cynicism. How many times must he have heard similar pep-talks, before how many shows which had vanished without trace? He no longer had any expectations of anything; he knew too much about the injustice and fickleness of the entertainment business to believe in any other power than that of luck.

He would work himself to death to make the show work, so long as no one asked him to believe in it. Even Charles, who was hardly a Little Noddy in his world-view, found something shocking in the depth of the man's cynicism.

Walter Proud, discreetly wishing to maintain a good producer/director relationship, suggested diffidently to Wayland Ogilvie that they should have a straight read-through on the clock to get some idea of how the show ran, unless of course Wayland wanted to approach it a different way. No, Wayland said, he was happy to do it that way, though on the first day of rehearsal he tended to try to picture the overall impact of the programme than get too involved in the script.

So they started. Charles still had a blind spot about television comedy material; he couldn't tell what was funny and what wasn't, and, having seen the miracles Lennie Barber had wrought with very indifferent lines in the barbershop sketch, he felt even less qualified to judge. However, Steve Clinton laughed raucously at every joke and there seemed to be sycophantic titters from the production crew from time to time, so maybe this was funny too.

The trouble was that Charles didn't have Lennie Barber's performance and reactions to help in his response. It soon became apparent that the comedian could not read. Not that he was illiterate, but that he couldn't sightread and give a performance at the same time. Charles hadn't met enough comedians to know how common a failing this is. Performers used to working seasoned material or adding new jokes and ad libs in the skirmishing of night club work are very rarely depen-dent on scripts and can be seriously thrown by trying to give life to words on the printed page.

Charles' first reaction was one of fear, that Barber

was not going to improve and that this stumbling, ill-timed performance would be the one presented to the studio audience. He rationalised that fear away. Obviously, once he had learnt the script, the comedian would start to build his performance, start to characterise and time the lines. But Barber's inept read-through, particularly when all of the minor comedy supports were giving extravagantly self-indulgent (but funny) cameos, seemed to get the project off to a bad start.

It was also apparent as they read that the star didn't like a lot of the script. He kept stopping on jokes, shaking his head and looking up to Walter Proud as if to start discussion, but on each occasion the producer gestured that the readthrough should continue and points be raised later. Charles had got the impression that there had already been meetings between Proud, Barber and the writers when rewrites had been demanded, and the whole show (or certainly the bits that Barber appeared in—he showed no interest in the rest) looked like being rewritten a good bit more before the recording day arrived.

They reached the end of the script and Lennie Barber, in spite of his mood, sang through a verse and chorus of the closing song, the signature tune of the old *Barber and Pole Show, Who Cares About Tomorrow When Tonight is Now?*

Walter Proud leant across to look over the PA Theresa's shoulder at her stopwatch. 'Just about right for time too. Lovely read. Thank you all—sorry, Wayland, I should let you speak first.'

'No, don't worry. I'm just kind of trying to visualise the overall shape of the conception.'

'Thank you, Wayland. No, I'd really like to say I think we're really on to something very, very big.'

'Not without some changes we're not,' stated Lennie Barber baldly.

'What do you mean, Lennie?' asked Walter heartily, as if he could will away the dissonant voice. But he had started to sweat. The moment when a star says he's unhappy with the script is the one that every producer fears, breeder of many coronaries.

'I mean, Walter, that a lot of this stuff is just wrong. There are things in here that I can't do. For example, that sketch where I go into the chemist and ask for a take-away poltergeist—'

'That's a bloody good sketch,' objected Paul Royce.

'That I don't know. It may be good, it may be bad; all I know is that it's wrong for me. I can't play that sort of material.'

'Oh, come on, Lennie,' Walter cajoled. 'You don't know until you've tried.'

'I know.'

Paul Royce looked petulant. 'I thought the idea of this show was to try out something new, to bring you up to date.'

'Try out something new, yes. But I'm still Lennie Barber. It's got to be new material, but new Lennie Barber material. I haven't spent a lifetime building up my own comic identity to have it thrown over like this. Listen, that sketch might go all right in Monty Python or whatever it's called—'

'Oh, so you don't think Monty Python's funny?' asked Paul Royce, leading Barber into a pit of impossibly reactionary depths.

'That's not the issue. I think they do that sort of stuff very well. And I damned well know that I'd do it very badly. I've got to work to my strengths, not show myself up by trying to do things other people do a lot better.'

Paul Royce's lip curled. 'Well, if you're never going to try anything new . . .'

Walter Proud came in quickly, placating. 'Don't worry. We'll have a look at that sketch.'

'Not have a look at it—cut it.'

'We'll see, Lennie, we'll see. Now if we can get on. I had a few points which—'

'There's a whole lot more too,' said Lennie Barber. 'Stuff that's going to have to be changed.'

Everyone looked at the comedian with annoyance. He was not making himself popular. And yet Charles found his respect for the man increasing. Having seen Barber work, he knew the fine instinct that made him function as a comedian. If he said he wasn't happy with the material, the chances were that he was right. He could only work efficiently with jokes he trusted.

Ignoring the wall of cold looks around him, Lennie continued. 'A lot of it's far too up-market for me, anyway.'

Paul Royce was again offended. 'What do you mean—up-market? You should never underestimate your audience. They understand more than you give them credit for.'

'It's not a matter of whether they understand it; it's whether they expect to hear it from me. I mean, for example, that joke about Oedipus doing the week's shopping down at Mothercare.'

'That's a bloody good joke,' snapped Paul Royce. 'Just because you've never heard of Oedipus—'

'Of course I've bloody heard of Oedipus. He killed his father, Laius, King of Thebes, and married his mother, Jocasta, but that is not the point. The audience would not expect the Lennie Barber they remember to tell a joke like that.'

'That's assuming any of them remember Lennie Barber at all,' riposted Paul Royce venomously.

Walter Proud rushed in with his can of oil for troubled waters, which is standard issue equipment for all producers. To shift the mood of the conversation, he brought in the director. 'What's your feeling on this, Wayland?'

'I don't know.' The dreamy eyes behind gold-rimmed glasses came back lazily from their reverie. 'I was just trying to paint a picture of that final monologue. I think we should probably shoot it through something. Ferns, maybe. With the set almost burnt-out behind.'

Charles got the feeling that *The New Barber and Pole*

*Show* would not be a completely trouble-free production.

There was a pay-phone in the corridor outside the Drill Hall and he went to it in a rehearsal break. Through the arguments over the script, he had been formulating his next move in the case of Bill Peaky's murder.

A girl answered. 'Miffy Turtle Agency.'

Her voice was Cockney. They were all Cockney —Miffy, Carla, the late Bill Peaky. But the feeling they all gave Charles was not of lovable, Dickensian Cockneys, rather of potentially criminal, Kray Brothers type of Cockneys. Miffy particularly, with his solid frame and his flashy jewellery, seemed only one step from a gangster.

'Could I speak to Mr Turtle, please?'

'Who wants him?'

'My name is Charles Paris.'

' 'Ang on a minute.' Silence. A click. 'You're through.'

'Hello, Charles. What can I do you for?'

'Miffy, I wondered if I could come and talk to you.'

'What about?'

'Well, it's about my working with Lennie Barber. I mean, you represent him, don't you?'

'Yeah.'

'Well, the fact is . . .' Time for a little tactical disloyalty. 'I've been with the same agent for some years and I can't honestly say he does a lot for me. '(That bit, at least, was true.) 'I was thinking, if this partnership with Lennie develops into anything, there might be arguments for us being jointly represented.'

'You might have a point.' Miffy didn't sound too bowled over by the idea. 'Of course, I do specialise in the variety area. Clubs, summer season, panto, that sort of scene.'

'Yes, well, that seems to be the way my career's moving at the moment.' Absolute lies, Charles thought

as he said it. On the other hand, it was moving more in
that direction than it was in any other. In every other
area of the entertainment business its customary stasis
obtained.

'OK. Come and have a talk about it. Fill me in a bit
on what you done and so on. We'll see if an
arrangement is going to be mutually beneficial. How're
you placed?'

'As you know, we've just started rehearsals for the
telly. But I think there's going to be some kind of script
conference this afternoon that won't involve me. So I'll
be free later.'

'OK. Come along about four then. You know where
we are?'

'Yes.'

'The name's not on the door yet, 'cause we only just
moved, but when you get here, it's second floor.'

The new address of the Miffy Turtle Agency was,
Charles decided, a step up in the world. It was in Argyll
Street, just next to the London Palladium, maybe in the
hope that success would rub off by contiguity. Miffy
Turtle obviously had hopes of expansion to afford such
an address; it also explained his anxiety at the prospect
of losing his most lucrative clients.

The move had been very recent. The reception area
was littered with half-emptied boxes and piled-up
folders. The girl behind the typewriter looked as
Cockney as she had sounded on the phone. Sharp, pert
little face, sharp, pert little body. The sort of girl you'd
never dare make a pass at for fear she'd laugh at you.

'Mr Paris, innit? OK, I'll just go in and see if Miffy's
free.' She went through the door to an inner office and
returned after a brief exchange. 'Won't keep you a
minute. Take a seat.'

He could hear a low hum of conversation from the office. It sounded like a female voice with Miffy's. A large
framed poster leaning against the wall prompted
visions of a leggy chorus girl and Charles fantasised a

little as to what would come out of the office. In a rather adolescent way, he had built up an image of Variety work as sexier than legitimate theatre.

But he couldn't indulge in such fantasies; it was more important to prepare himself for the approaching interview.

It struck him that he was in danger of becoming a joke figure for his repeated murder accusations. Like a pimply youth proposing to every woman he meets, he seemed constantly to be gearing himself up to another confrontation. Janine Bentley, Paul Royce, now Miffy Turtle. Thank God he felt confident that he was finally on the right track. If this proved to be another mare's nest, he would look ridiculous. He decided that in future murder investigations (if any) he should try to avoid confrontations. Just build up a dossier of evidence and then hand it over to the police. Though, in this case, there would be a hell of a lot of explaining to do before he could get down to detail and, from his own experience, the police welcomed amateur detectives about as avidly as elephants welcome umbrella-stand manufacturers.

Something buzzed on the girl's desk and she ushered him into Miffy's office. Charles did a slight take when he saw that the agent was alone. There was another door facing his desk, which must lead to another exit. The fantasy chorus girl had gone that way.

In spite of the chaos in the outer office, efforts had been made to put Miffy Turtle in a setting worthy of a West End agent, or at least the setting in which West End agents appear in West End plays. He sat in a swivel chair upholstered in dark brown leather. Across the large mahogany desk his clients were offered a matching reproduction Chesterfield. On the wall there were framed photographs of people Charles didn't recognise, girls in sequinned dresses, men with big bow ties, all with insincere smiles and insincere messages scrawled across them. Either side of the window red velvet curtains hung, the skimpiness of their cut suggesting that they were not designed ever to be pulled.

Miffy maintained the image. He wore a pale green three-piece suit; the heavy gold cuff-links and chunky identity bracelet were very much in evidence. He looked like a footballer giving a pre-match interview.

To Charles it all seemed wrong. In his experience the really big agents worked from dusty garrets or anonymous boxes. Dickie Peck, one of the most important of the lot, had an office as musty and in need of decoration as the bar of a provincial rep.

Miffy rose expansively and gestured to the Chesterfield. As close as this, Charles was very aware of his adversary's powerful build. A little chill spread over him at the thought of what he was about to do.

'Glad you could come so soon, Charles. Like a cup of tea, eh?'

'Thank you.'

Miffy pressed the switch of his intercom and gave the order. The self-conscious way he used the machine confirmed the impression given by its glossy exterior. He had kitted himself out with the complete set of props when he moved into the office.

'Nice place.' Charles said it to gain a little time and because he thought he might as well at least start on a friendly basis.

Miffy glowed. 'Yes, I'm pleased with it. I've always had this theory that if you're going to move into the big league, you got to look as if you're there already.'

'Not a bad principle. And you are moving into the big league?'

'Sure I am. Whole scene needs a shake-up. All the top names in the agency business are old men now. Need a bit of young blood. It's wide open.'

'Good.'

'Good for my clients, yes. Now, like I said on the phone, I only deal with Variety stuff. Fine while you're with Lennie doing that sort of work, but if the calls start coming through from the Royal Bloody Shakespeare Company, I wouldn't know where to begin.'

'The Royal Bloody Shakespeare Company has managed to do without my services for the past eleven years and I doubt if they're planning a major policy switch.'

'No, I was speaking, like, generally. I mean, that's what you are basically, an actor, isn't it?'

'I suppose so.' Charles hesitated. He was feeling uncomfortable. He could go on with this banter indefinitely, but if he didn't make some sort of move soon, he was going to walk out in ten minutes under contract to the man he had come to accuse. He blurted out, 'I've come about Bill Peaky.'

'Bill Peaky.' Miffy looked bewildered.

'Yes. I know he was murdered.'

'Murdered.' Again the repetition sound genuinely flummoxed. But Charles did not have a chance to assess the reaction. He heard the soft click of a door behind him and saw Miffy Turtle's eyes rise, puzzled, to the person who had just come in.

Charles turned to find himself looking up the barrel of a small black pistol at the end of which was a tight-lipped Carla.

Miffy spoke first. 'What the hell are you doing, love?'

Her voice had entirely lost its elocuted veneer. 'It's all right, Miff. I should have told you before. He came sniffing round the house with this murder story, but I thought I'd thrown him off your scent. Now it looks like we're going to have to keep him quiet.'

She waved the gun vaguely, but not vaguely enough to be reassuring. 'Now, please, Mrs Pratt,' Charles remonstrated.

'Keep still. I don't know how he worked it out, Miff, but you must've made some mistake, not cleared your tracks properly. What are we going to do with him?'

'I don't bloody know.' The agent sounded extremely confused. He had not started the afternoon with any plans for silencing and disposing of the bodies of men who knew too much and his mind was taking a little while to accommodate the idea.

'How did you find it out, Mr Paris?' asked Carla, the gun still describing unsettling pirouettes in her hand.

'Various things. I found out that Miffy hadn't been in your husband's dressing room during the interval on the day he died. That Dickie Peck was set to steal your husband as a client. And then I . . . discovered that you two were lovers. So I put two and two together.'

'And got bloody seventeen.' Miffy Turtle was through his confused stage and a definable mood had now emerged. That mood was extreme anger. 'I don't know what you're talking about. Murder? What is this? Are you rehearsing for a play or something? Or is it some bloody stupid practical joke? 'Cause the humour's wearing a bit thin and I—'

Carla silenced him. 'Miffy, don't bother. You're not going to persuade him off it now he's got the idea into his head. We got to decide what to do with him. If he goes to the police—'

'If he goes to the police, they'll laugh their bloody heads off and tell him not to waste their time. Good God, Carla, d'you really believe I killed Bill?'

'Well . . .'

'Go on, do you?'

She faced her lover defiantly. 'All right. Yes, I do. And what's more, I don't care. I don't love you less for it. In fact, I love you more. To think you would do that for me, to think you were prepared to get that little creep out of my life so that we could be together . . . I'll do whatever you say. What are we going to do about him?' She pointed the gun at Charles.

Miffy was silent. When he spoke, his voice was cold. 'Listen, Carla. One, I don't believe Bill was murdered. Two, if he was, I didn't do it.'

She broke the ensuing silence, but didn't get far before he snapped back at her savagely. 'And let me tell you that to hear you thought me capable of murdering him is the worst news I've had for some long time. Good God, I thought we knew each other, trusted each other.'

'But you kept saying you wished he was out of the way. You said you wanted us to get married and—'

'Yes, I said that. Whether I still mean it after this afternoon I'm not so sure. But I meant I wanted him to divorce you. I am not a killer, Carla.'

Suddenly she broke. Her lover's anger destroyed her and she sank weeping to the floor. The gun dropped noisily beside her.

Miffy didn't go to help. He looked coldy at Charles, who had been ignored through the preceding exchange and said, with some dignity, 'I think you'd better leave my office.'

'No, I'm sorry. I came here certain that you killed Bill Peaky and you still haven't given me any reason to change my opinion. You certainly had the motive and you had the opportunity. Unless you can provide yourself with an alibi for the whole of the interval, I'm still not going to be satisfied.'

'All right.' Miffy Turtle sounded dangerously grim. 'I took Dickie bloody Peck round to Bill's dressing room. I then went to find one of the dancers who was ill. She hadn't appeared in the first half closer and I wanted to know why. I had money in that show; I was concerned about the production.'

'The girl was Janine Bentley?' Charles knew the answer, but still asked the question.

'Yes. I found her with the theatre St. John's Ambulance man and stayed with her until a taxi came to take her home.'

So there it was—back to Harry, the St John's Ambulance man. Checkable, certainly. But fairly convincing. Unless Janine and Miffy were in league. Unless the St. John's Ambulance man had killed Peaky. Charles suddenly felt very tired and very much like a man on the eve of his fifty-first birthday. 'I'll check your alibi,' he said defiantly, but without conviction.

'You bloody check it. And think yourself lucky I haven't knocked your bloody block off.'

Charles rose with what dignity he could muster. He

was almost at the door when Miffy spoke again. His voice had softened now and was musing, curious. 'Do you really think Bill was murdered?'

Charles nodded.

'Good God.' Miffy shook his head sadly. 'I knew he was unpopular, but I didn't think anyone . . .' He stopped. 'Unless . . .'

'Yes?' Charles was alert for any clues to help him out of the confusion which was building up inside his head.

'Only one person I know might have done it.'

'Hmm?' He tried not to sound too eager.

'I don't know. I probably shouldn't say it, but I did hear him having an argument with Bill. Also he's a junkie, so I shouldn't think he knows what he's doing when he's had a fix. Hmm. I don't know.'

'Who are you talking about?'

'Boy called Chox Morton. Roadie with Mixed Bathing.'

'And you say he's on drugs?'

'Sure. Silly little bugger. Heroin. He won't be around two years from now, I bet. Killing himself.'

'And he had an argument with Bill Peaky?'

'Yes. Needless to say, he was very secretive about the drugs thing. I found out by accident and he was in a terrible state, making me swear never to tell anyone. He was terrified of being handed over to the police. Not afraid of going to prison or anything like that, just terrified of being taken away from his fix. It didn't concern me, so I said I'd keep quiet about it. Unfortunately Bill also found out and he was less willing to keep his mouth shut.'

'He did go to the police?'

'No, no, that wasn't Bill's way. He was a nasty little sod. He liked having power over people. Girls, in particular, but everyone. To have a secret about someone and hold it over them, he liked that. That's what he would have done with his knowledge of Chox's addiction.' Miffy was silent for a moment. 'However he went, the world's well rid of him.'

This remark induced a new burst of crying from Carla, still lying on the floor behind the Chesterfield. Miffy looked over in her direction, but did not move. The lovers had a lot of talking to do, if they were to salvage their relationship.

And Charles Paris was going to have to do a lot of thinking.

# Chapter XIII

COMIC: It's a really rough area—if you see a cat
with a tail on round there you know it's a
tourist.

'Good God, Charles. Every time you ring me up you've
got a new suspect.'

'I've been through a few since we last spoke.'

'Well, I hope you're being a good little amateur detective and checking out all these supposed alibis.
Somebody capable of murder is not going to baulk at
telling the odd lie to get them off the hook.'

'From your tone I gather you've done Janine's alibi.'

'I have actually. I spent a long afternoon on the
phone yesterday checking out Harry, the St. John's Ambulance man in Hunstanton. It took me a long time to
find him—I started with the theatre and kept getting
new numbers. Tracked him down to his sister's in
Lowestoft where he was having anchovy paste sandwiches with the crusts cut off. Chatty old boy, you may
gather. Anyway, he remembered the occasion perfectly
and confirmed that Janine had been with him right
through the interval. Together with Miffy Turtle.'

'You just asked him like that?'

'No, I was a bit subtle. I implied it was a legal matter
of urgency and discretion and that members of the
Royal Family were not uninvolved. The old boy was
very flattered to be asked. Got quite excited about it.'

'I see. So, as I thought, those two are out of the running.'

'It's all very well to say "as I thought". True detective work is the product of endless painstaking research, of enquiry and counter-enquiry.'

'So I've heard. Maybe that's why I'm not a true detective. Mind you, I think I'm getting somewhere this time.'

'With Suspect Number 348? This boy called Chips.'

'Chox.'

'All the people in this case have such ridiculous names.'

'That's show business, Gerald. Anyway, Chox is certainly a strange piece of work. If he is a drug addict, it explains quite a lot about him. Yes.'

This last word was spoken with a sudden insight, which prompted Gerald to ask, 'Yes what?'

'I've just thought of something else. Heroin addicts inject into their forearms, don't they?'

'I don't know. Not exactly the circles I move in, Charles.'

'I'm sure they do. Anyway, when I grabbed the boy's arm a couple of days ago, he reacted pretty violently. Said he was afraid I was queer and he'd had nasty experiences that way, but thinking about it now, I reckon I'd hurt his arm or he was afraid I'd pull his sleeve up and expose him. I think junkies get pretty secretive about their addiction. Read something somewhere that that's part of the attraction, a kind of self-punishment, death-wish thing. That's why they often inject themselves in squalid places, lavatories and so on. And why they sometimes deliberately use infected needles.'

'This wealth of detail is a fascinating insight into the circles *you* move in, Charles.'

'Oh come on, Gerald, you're a solicitor. You must come up against drugs cases from time to time.'

'I'm pleased to say that the only occasion I have come up against one was when the teenage son of a titled client of mine was found to have marijuana on his person. At Ascot.'

'I might have guessed. And no doubt you got him off on the grounds that he was reacting against a nanny who'd always told him to keep off the grass.'

'Something like that, yes.'

'Anyway, I'm going to find out a bit more about Mr Chox Morton. If what Miffy Turtle said was true, he had a motive—and I must say, that business about Bill Peaky liking to have holds over people confirms the impression I had got of his character. He does seem to have been a really unpleasant bit of work. I wasn't sure for a bit, because his wife painted such a different picture, but now I've discovered she was lying, the verdict seems to be more or less unanimous.'

'You're rambling, Charles.'

'Sorry. Just working it out for my own benefit. Yes, Chox had a motive all right. He also had the knowledge to commit the crime. He was better qualified than anyone, knew that sound system inside out, would have heard about the old theatre electrician dying, no problem. It's funny.'

'What?' asked Gerald, exasperated at Charles long stream-of-consciousness monologue.

'When I last saw him, Chox raised the subject of Peaky's death. Quite unprompted. Said how he had described the electrocution process to some of the company. I think perhaps in a twisted way he was boasting about the crime, crowing at the fact that he had got away with it.'

'Or perhaps he was testing, trying to find out how much you knew, how far you were behind him.'

'No. I'm sure he doesn't know I'm even investigating. Lennie Barber's the only one in the case who knows anything about my futile hobby. Him and Walter Proud.'

'I see. How's the show going, by the way?'

'Somewhat jerkily. Nothing gets rehearsed for more

than thirty seconds before Barber wants to change it. Then there's a long discussion where he agrees with everyone that he's going to be doing something different in the show. We start rehearsing again and he wants to change another line back to a hoary old joke which went down very well in the fifties. Classic comedian's insecurity, I guess. Terrified of anything new.'

'How are the writers reacting?'

'Pretty badly. Steve Clinton roars with laughter and cracks fatuous jokes; Paul Royce wanders around like Hamlet and keeps staging dramatic walkouts. The trouble is that Barber has no respect for writers at all. He comes from a tradition where you didn't have them, or, if you did, they were something you didn't mention, like bad breath. All in all, it doesn't make for the easiest working atmosphere.'

'Can't wait to see the show. I'll be there.'

'It'll probably all be marvellous. From what I've seen of him, Barber's instincts about material are usually right.'

'How's the director coping?'

'Oh, he walks around composing Rembrandts in his mind's eye and saying how he doesn't get on with Aquarians. The whole thing's a riot.'

'Sounds it.'

'Yes, I'm glad I've got a murder investigation to think about. Keeps my mind off the show.'

Rehearsals in the RNVR Drill Hall had broken down again. This time it had been over the line, 'It's like a quack doctor charging for worthless advice—a duck-billed platitude', which Lennie Barber felt (with, to Charles' mind, some justification) was neither very funny nor suited to his style of performance.

In the course of the row, Paul Royce walked out again, Steve Clinton said 'Keep your hair on—as the Commissioner said to Kojak' and laughed a lot, Wayland Ogilvie decided he had to go and have a conference with the designer about a rococo mirror and the

PA Theresa told two of the support characters that they should go and have wardrobe fittings.

The rehearsal being effectively over, Lennie Barber and Charles Paris went round to the pub (having first hidden behind a hedge until Steve Clinton had left the vicinity—a precaution which was becoming routine for everyone on the production).

The new Barber and Pole started in a determined way with large whiskies. 'How'd you reckon it's going, Lennie?'

'Death.'

'You don't think it's got a chance?'

'God knows. Depends how it goes on the night. And how many actual jokes we can get in instead of bloody university revue lines.'

'Do you want it to work?'

The old comedian looked at Charles in amazement. 'Of course I want it to work. What do you take me for?'

'I'm sorry. It's just that sometimes you seem so cynical, it's hard to believe that you have any real ambition.'

Lennie Barber's eyes flickered as he assessed this remark. 'Do I? Do I really do that, Charles? Yeah, I suppose I do.' He rubbed his thumb against the point of his chin reflectively. 'And if I do, my boy, it's very simply what a psychologist would call a defence mechanism. I don't want to tempt providence, but of course I want the bloody show to work, of course I want to be a star. What do you think it's been like for me, having been at the top, to slide slowly downwards? Every time I watched the bloody telly I'd see some new comic. At first it was blokes who'd been on the same bill as me when I'd toured the Number Ones—except they'd been way down the bill and I'd been the top. I think that was the worst bit really, when it was people I recognised, people I knew weren't as good as me. After a bit they were just faces that come on. I'd never seen any of them before and, as far as I was concerned, they all looked exactly the same. Styles changed a bit, different jokes

came round, but it was all the same really, and I knew I
could do better. Comedians nowadays, they're nothing
. . . Did you hear that great line Arthur Askey come up
with when Granada started that *Comedians* series. "I
see they've opened a new tin of Irish comics," he said.
That's what they all are now—prepackaged, inof-
fensive, characterless. OK, I sound like an old man wit-
tering on about things being better when I was young.
Well, I am an old man and, what's more, things bloody
were better when I was young. Comedy certainly was
better, Variety was. Television has taken the guts out of
everything. No rough edges, no . . . nothing.' He was
silent, then emptied his glass with a positive movement.
'But I want to come back, even if it means television.
Yes, I want this show to be a thumping great, enormous, copper-bottomed success.'

Charles felt closer to Lennie Barber at that moment
than he had since they had first met. Gone was the mask
of cynicism and the disquieting obsession with his
bowels; it was the real man who had been talking.

Barber looked at his watch. 'Better be off, I suppose.'

'Aren't we going to have another drink?' Charles was
reluctant to break the new mood between them.

'No, I don't think that I . . . Well . . .' The comedian
looked embarrassed. 'The fact is, I haven't got any
money with me. It's my round and I like to pay my
bit. Better be off, I think.'

'No. I'll get them.'

'But you got the last lot.'

'Don't be silly. Come on, while we're still both flush
with telly money.'

'Huh.' Barber seemed to be about to pass an opinion
on what he thought of telly money, but decided against
it. 'Look, tell you what . . . how about you lend me a
fiver and I get them and pay you back?'

'Fine.' Charles handed over the money and their
glasses were refilled. Barber took the change.

'Pay you back when I get to a bank.'

They sat companionably with their whisky. Charles

began to feel a glimmer of enthusiasm for the project. He liked the idea of working with Lennie Barber. And, if the show were anything like a success, it could be a very profitable partnership. His brief experience had taught him that Light Entertainment fees were considerably fatter than Drama ones. And then there were all the extras that that sort of work led to—club bookings, businessmen's lunches where large piles of notes were handed over in payment, commercials. Charles had always said that that sort of show business was not for him, but then he had never been offered it. Given the opportunities it could bring he might not take such a high moral tone.

Lennie Barber broke into his speculations. 'You got anywhere about Bill Peaky?'

'You mean the murder?'

'Yes. Last time you mentioned it you were trying to track down that girl Janine.'

'I found her. She didn't kill him.'

'Any idea who did then, Monsewer Poirot?'

Charles hesitated. He had to be careful to whom he confided his suspicions. On the other hand, he did need to find out more about Chox Morton, and Lennie Barber had been in the same company right through the summer. Besides, Charles trusted the comedian completely. He took the plunge and mentioned Chox's name.

'Really? Well, he certainly had the technical knowledge.' Lennie Barber screwed up his face and reviewed the suggestion. 'Yeah, but why?'

'Did you know he was on drugs?'

'Yes, I did actually. Silly little bugger. Good God, there are enough natural things around to shorten your life without adding to them. I used to drink—I mean really drink—so I suppose I know a bit what it's about. What, you reckon he just got high and didn't know what he was doing?'

'No. Bill Peaky found out the drugs thing and threatened to shop him.'

'Did he? Well, surprise, surprise. Yes, that's true to form. Whoever did kill him, you know, did the world a great service.'

'I reckon Chox is highest on the list of possibles at the moment. If only I could get some sort of evidence, if only someone had seen him on the stage during the interval . . . Lennie, you know that theatre. Do you reckon he could've fixed the wiring without anyone seeing him?'

'Yes, I'm sure he could. For a start, the first thing anyone onstage does when the first half curtain comes down is get off. Go to their dressing rooms, cup of tea in the Green Room, whatever. So it was very unlikely anyone would be around to see him.

'Except Norman del Rosa doing his Peeping Tom act.'

'But surely he'd have mentioned if he had seen anyone apart from Peaky.'

'I suppose so.'

'And even if anyone had seen Chox, I don't reckon they'd have thought twice about it, Charles. He was always wandering about the place with cables under his arm. Part of the furniture. Added to which nobody'd be looking for anything suspicious, anyway. You forget that you're the only person who thinks of this thing as murder.'

'Well, me and about half of the cast of the show who I've so far accused of doing it.'

'Yeah, but nobody suspected murder at the time. By now they'd have forgotten what happened a month ago.' The comedian's forehead wrinkled, then cleared. 'I have thought of something, though. If he did want to be onstage unnoticed while he sorted the wiring out, he could have gone into the lighting store.'

'That was actually onstage?'

'Yeah, everything all higgledy-piggledy in that place. It was just in the wings. That's where the faulty cable come from anyway. Also, thing about that was it had a lock on the door, 'cause of the expensive gear they kept

there. I used to reckon Chox sometimes went in there to
give himself a fix.'

'Yes,' Charles interpolated excitedly, 'that must have
been it. Because I remember now, Miffy Turtle said the
lock had gone on the Gents that day. So if Chox wanted
to hide away, he'd have had to go to the lighting store.'

'Right. Yeah, I reckon that's what he must've done.
Not that we can prove it. So it doesn't really help
much.'

'Mmm.' The inevitable was looming large in front of
Charles. 'So, if there's no likelihood of my finding any
evidence, I guess that means another confrontation.'

'Maybe. I wonder.'

'You have another idea?'

'I don't know. Just a thought. You see, I got to know
Chox quite well while we was down in Hunstanton. I
don't mean I got close to him—I don't think anyone did
that, but I think he kind of trusted me. I wonder if we
were to talk to him together . . . I've a feeling he might
be more forthcoming that way, relax a bit, you know.
What do you say?'

'Sounds a great idea to me.' Anything rather than
steeling himself to another solo encounter with a supposed murderer.

'Well, look—What's the time? Hmm. I got to go
back to see Walter, try and get some more of this bloody
script sorted out. So that'll take . . . I don't know, three
bloody years to get it anything like respectable. But let's
say till seven. Can you meet me round Chox's place
about eight?'

'Sure. Where's he live?'

Barber gave an address in North Kensington. 'I'll ring
him first to check he's going to be in. You ring Walter's
office in a couple of hours and I'll be able to confirm
that. Otherwise, see you there at eight.'

Charles arrived shortly after eight. The road in North
Kensington had been built for prosperous Victorians,
but now the trees which lined it were scraped and scabby

and the tall façades of the houses diseased by neglect. Paint flaked from porticoes, toothless balcony railings gaped, overflow pipes scored green smears down walls and the doorsteps were littered with dustbins and old magazines. A dusty cortège of outmoded Fords, some wheelless, some lividly splodged with aerosol paint, lined the gutter. The aerosol artist had also left his blurred testimony on the trees and every bit of wall that he could reach.

The large front door out of which Lennie Barber emerged had been slashed with lines of spray paint, silver mocking the dirty blue beneath.

'I was waiting just inside the hall, Charles. Not the sort of area to hang about in. Lot of muggings round here. Also not too many friendly white faces, know what I mean?'

Charles nodded and followed Barber into the dimly-lit hall. The outline of what had once been an impressive sweep of stairs emerged from the gloom ahead. But its classical proportions had been distorted by the random juttings of hardboard walls with which the fine old house had been converted into bedsitters.

'Like I said, Charles, when you rang, he's expecting us. I said you was coming. He didn't sound suspicious or anything. I think he may have just had a fix. Didn't sound all there. If he's still in the state, it might be good for us. He'll be relaxed and talk. Then we'll find out what really did happen.'

'Let's hope so.'

The push-button time-switch in the hall produced no more light. Either the bulbs had been nicked or just not replaced by absentee landlords. As Charles and Barber groped their way up the banister, they became aware of the smell of the house—a compound of used cooking oil, beer and wet cardboard. Reggae music and softly accented voices issued from behind the doors of the other bedsitters they passed.

On the second landing Charles paused to let Barber catch up with him. The comedian was breathing heavily, suddenly an old man. Struggling for his breath, he leant against the banister and gestured straight ahead through the murk. 'It's that one,' he gasped.

The door was slightly ajar, but no light showed through the crack. Charles knocked softly. Then harder. Harder again. Nothing.

Struck by an abrupt sense of panic, he pushed the door open with his left hand and with the right reached round for the light switch.

He felt its outline and the pain hit him. As his fingers stung with the snapping flash of electricity, he had a vision of Bill Peaky's wild face as he had grasped the microphone in Hunstanton. At the same time the impact of the shock slammed him backwards against the banister.

## Chapter XIV

FEED: There's a man outside with a nasty look on his face.
COMIC: Tell him you've already got one.

Charles felt as if some demonic barman had mixed him with ice and fire and was determined to shake him into the cocktail of all time.

Lennie Barber was crouching over him, his face old and anxious in the half-light. 'You all right? What happened?' he kept repeating.

After a bit, Charles decided that he wasn't that badly hurt. His fingers still stung and his arm felt numb. The impact with which he had met the banisters was going to leave a great bruised line across his back. But basically, he would survive.

'I'll be OK, Lennie. Help me up.'

It hurt, but he could walk. He rubbed his tingling wrist and moved across to the door of Chox's bedsitter again. There was still silence from inside. From the other doors on the landing there were human sounds, but no one had come out to see what had caused the crash. Perhaps the sounds of violence were too familiar to be investigated. Perhaps it was wiser to keep out of other people's troubles.

Charles felt confident that Chox's room was empty and went in. After a bit of fumbling in the dark, he found a bedside lamp of the Chianti bottle variety that went out of fashion in the fifties, and switched it on.

The room was a terrible mess. A mattress on the floor served as a bed and hadn't been made for some weeks. The floor was littered with copies of *Melody Maker, New Musical Express* and other less-established music papers. In the gaps these left, LP sleeves poked through. Encrusted coffee cups were marooned among the flotsam.

He moved across to the light switch, aware of Lennie Barber's frightened face peering round the door-frame. The booby trap had been simple. Chox had merely taken off the plastic cover of the switch and pulled out the wires so that they would be the first thing a reaching hand would meet. Simple, but efficient.

Charles became aware of what Lennie Barber was saying. 'I shouldn't have told him.'

'Shouldn't have told him what?'

'Shouldn't have told him you were coming. Charles. Someone must have mentioned that you had this sideline as an amateur detective and he must have realised you were on to him.'

'I suppose so.'

'He intended to kill you, Charles. God, it's just struck me. If I hadn't been such a short-winded old fart, I could have been the first one into that room.'

'Yes. Just a minute.' A new thought.

'What?'

'You don't think Chox is out to get you, do you?'

'What do you mean?'

'I was just thinking back to the accident you had in Hunstanton. When you burnt your hands. Had Chox been round to your digs?'

'He had, but—'

'It's possible that he'd sabotaged your kettle. He seems to have an unhealthy interest in murder by electrical accident.'

'Yes. You had a lucky escape, Charles.'

'Maybe. Of course, the switch wasn't certain to kill me. As I have proved by standing here before you now.'

'No. Maybe he just wanted to warn you.'

'What do you mean?'

'To discourage you. To indicate that, if you go on hounding him he'll try something a bit less hit-and-miss.'

Suddenly the electric shock seemed to be on him again and Charles shivered uncontrollably. 'Do you know,' he managed to say, 'at the moment I feel very inclined to take the hint. Let's go and have an extremely large drink.'

Fortunately he didn't have much time over the next few days to examine the ethics of the case. In the brief moments when it loomed into his mind, the questions it posed were quite simple: do I want to go on pursuing Chox Morton or can I be content with the intellectual satisfaction of knowing that he killed Bill Peaky? (There was now no doubt about this last assertion; the booby-trapping of the light switch was tantamount to an admission.) Does Bill Peaky's death matter anyway, since he was such an unpleasant person? Or is the world just rid of another bastard? Do I believe in an Ultimate Truth, which must always be upheld?

And each time Charles answered the final question: no. Having reached his solution, he felt no urgency to bring the culprit to justice. He now recognised Chox's warning for what it was and decided to heed it. Further inquisitiveness might not get off so lightly.

But the peace he achieved with this *nolle prosequi* decision was never complete. He could not forget that he was the possessor of secret knowledge about Chox Morton and it had been for just such knowledge that Bill Peaky had died.

However, as rehearsals for *The New Barber and Pole Show* picked up pace, he had little time for such gloomy thoughts. The actual rehearsing was tiring, but the constant breaks for script carpentry were even more exhausting. Every change meant learning completely different lines (or slightly different lines, which was

worse). Walter Proud was constantly being summoned
from his office to make peace between Lennie Barber
and the writers as another of their original gems was
replaced by a joke long past pensionable age. Wayland
Ogilvie, who had no interest in the words at all (or indeed the performances; he would have been quite happy
photographing bowls of fruit so long as he was allowed
to do it artistically), kept complaining that the changes
were ruining the composition of his pictures and
fulminating quietly against Aquarians. The Stage
Manager muttered evilly as props were cut and new ones
suddenly required. Generally, Lennie Barber was not
making himself the most popular person around the
production.

And yet Charles did not lose his respect for the old
comedian; he still felt sure Barber's instincts were right.
The trouble was that, while Barber had an exact image
of his own comic persona and knew instantly what
material fitted it and what didn't, he was not articulate
enough in talking about comedy to explain his reasons.
He would just stop when he came to a line that wasn't
right and could not go on until it had been changed.

There was nothing prima donna-ish about these constant breaks in the rehearsal; he seemed genuinely to
regret his inability to say the lines; but nothing would in-
duce him to take them on trust and try them out on the
studio audience.

'We can always edit it out if it doesn't get the laugh,
love,' Wayland Ogilvie would say in a bored voice.

'Of course it'll get the laugh,' Paul Royce would ob-
ject heatedly. 'It's a bloody good line.'

'It may be a bloody good line, but it's not a Lennie
Barber line,' the comedian would reason patiently
before Paul Royce once again flung himself out of the
room.

There was one oasis of calm in the turmoil of rehearsals. It was another barbershop sketch which had been
taken intact from the original Barber and Pole music

hall act. The set-up was as before and so were the catch-phrases, but the jokes were different. Still as corny as in the other sketch and still, handled by Lennie Barber, magic. Again he directed Charles in the timing of the piece, leaving Wayland Ogilvie mouthing at the corner of the Drill Hall. Charles knew the sketch could not fail to work and that, given time to tailor and familiarise himself with the new material, Barber could be brilliant throughout and make a sensational comeback.

But television schedules are tight and there was only a fortnight of rehearsal for the fifty-minute programme. With constant interruptions for rewrites, as well as the depravations of costume fittings, design conferences and so on, there was just not going to be enough time.

Charles was not involved a great deal in the show, in spite of his grandiose billing in the title. He did the barbershop sketch and a couple of other quick items as Wilkie Pole. The rest of the time was filled by modern sketches featuring Lennie Barber and the team of comedy supports, an opening and closing monologue by the comedian and two guest spots.

The guests were a dance group (not in fact These Foolish Things, but totally indistinguishable from them) and a French singer whose big sad eyes and cloying romanticism won the adulation of agoraphobic housewives and the detestation of their red-blooded British husbands. Because of the tight schedule these two items were to be prerecorded the day before and played in to the studio audience.

The dancers presented no problem. They just came in and did the Chuck Sheba dance to their prerecorded vocal and music tracks, thus filling another three minutes of television time with viewzak.

But the French singer needed introducing. He was a guest on the show and Walter Proud was keen to have show business guests right through the (conjectural) series, so Lennie Barber had to learn how to give schmaltzy show business introductions. This part of the show probably caused more scripting problems than any other. Lennie Barber did not have the natural fulsomeness of the well-loved television personality at the awards lunch and the French singer's agent turned down flat the idea of an insulting intro (which would have been the comedian's natural style). Eventually a compromise was reached and the introduction was rewritten into a little sketch for Barber and Pole.

The French singer came into vision and Lennie Barber did not recognise him and kept getting his name wrong. Wilkie Pole knew who the man was and was acutely embarrassed by his partner's ignorance and rudeness. After some linguistic byplay, Lennie Barber finally pronounced the guest's name correctly (whereupon, on the night, the Floor Manager would cue applause from the studio audience).

The result of this was that Lennie Barber and Charles Paris were required in the studio on the day before the main recording.

The French singer proved to be arrogant and humourless, but the little introductory sketch was recorded satisfactorily after the usual long camera rehearsal, false starts, retakes, cutaway shots, etc. As it turned out, Lennie could have delivered a really vicious introduction, since the French singer seemed to have no English except for the tortured words of the song he sang (and from the way he sang it, he didn't even understand them).

Charles and Lennie sat on the audience seats while the Frenchman mimed through a rehearsal of his song. He got involved in an altercation with Wayland Ogilvie, which seemed, so far as one could judge from the copious gestures, to be about which of his profiles was the better. Charles and Lennie stopped watching.

'Do you get any excitement, Lennie, sitting here, where the audience is going to sit tomorrow and see you perform?'

'Excitement, no. Nothing. Not in a television studio.
You don't get any feel of the audience when you've got
all those cameras and monitors in the way. Now if this
was a theatre, that'd be something else . . . I can never
sit in a theatre without getting a little flutter of excitement. I think it goes back to when I was a kid and
used to watch my old man from out front. Used to swell
up with pride before he come on, could hardly breathe.
I'd look round at all the people sitting there and I'd
think, They've all come to see him, and he's my Dad.
Still get that funny feeling in the theatre.'

An elegiac mood had descended on them. There was
no need to talk. Charles gazed round the studio, taking
in the glittery set, the enormous number of people
milling round the French singer, all the cameramen,
sound boom operators, floor managers, scene shifters,
make-up girls, prancing wardrobe assistants and grim-
faced men whose function was known only to their shop
stewards. He felt a slight tremor of fear. Television
always frightened him. In front of so many people,
apart from the audience, he never felt he could give a
natural performance.

He looked on up to the lights and monitors hanging
down from the grid. Then along the gallery that ran
round the top of the studio walls. Somebody was standing up there at the corner, looking straight down at him.

It was Chox Morton.

Charles touched Lennie's sleeve very gently. 'Don't
look suddenly, but Chox is up there.'

'Where?'

'In the lighting gallery.'

The comedian moved his head slowly until the
menacing, emaciated figure came into his line of vision.
'Shit. Yes. It looks like he doesn't think you were scared
off sufficiently!'

'If he's come to scare me a bit more, he's certainly
succeeding. What shall I do?'

'Look, you nip out of the studio through the control box. I'll go and have a word with him and tell him you've gone home.'

'He's hardly going to believe you. I'm still in make-up and costume.'

'He won't think of that.'

'You mean he thinks I normally go around in a red frock coat and red check trousers.'

'Leave it to me. If I keep him talking long enough, you'll have had time to get changed. But just stay in the back of the control box for about an hour. He'll have gone by then.'

'OK. I hope you are right. There's rather a lot of electrical equipment round this place. Paradise for a murderer like Chox.'

'Don't worry, the unions won't let him touch a thing. You can bet that in television there's a special union in charge of electrocution.'

'Ha bloody ha.'


Charles sat on a thickly upholstered seat in a small annexe separated by glass from the main control room. It was designed for the accommodation of television executives, foreign buyers, agents of very important artists and director's girl-friends, but now it was empty. No one wanted to watch the prerecording of an opening caption sequence on a Tuesday evening at eight o'clock.

He felt shivery and ill at ease. He trusted Lennie Barber, but suppose the comedian could not get to Chox, or suppose Chox didn't believe him about Charles' departure . . . He began to wonder, too late as usual, why the hell he got himself into these situations.

On the opposite wall of the control room was the bank of monitors which showed the views of the various cameras and Charles watched these in a desultory manner to pass the time. Only two of the cameras seemed to be doing anything relevant. They were making a complicated sequence of graphics, superimposed on slides, which kept breaking down because the two pictures would not stay exactly in line. Tempers in the box were fraying. Wayland Ogilvie kept bawling out the vision mixer and muttering sulphurous asides about Pisceans. The vision mixer snapped back angrily. Only the PA Theresa maintained her customary cool, calling shots with the unruffled poise of a metronome.

Charles found it difficult to get involved in the scene, and the time passed very slowly.

Then he caught sight of something on one of the monitors. It was a shot from a camera which was focused nowhere in particular, just framing the edge of the set. Behind this two figures were visible. Lennie Barber and Chox Morton.

There was no microphone boom near them, so, though Charles fiddled with the speaker controls in the little observation room, he could not hear what was being said.

But the mime was expressive enough. Lennie Barber was definitely telling Chox to go away. Chox seemed doubtful at first, then resigned, and the two parted.

Which was hopeful. If Chox believed Lennie's story about Charles having left the building, then the pressure was off for a little while at least. If only he could have actually heard what was being said between the two, Charles could have relaxed.

He was soon let off the hook. The door from the studio to the control room opened and Lennie Barber entered, followed by Walter Proud. The comedian came straight through to where Charles was sitting and whispered, 'It's all right. He's gone.'

'Thanks very much. Bless you, Lennie.'

Walter Proud bustled into the observation room, all jovial importance. 'Charles, Lennie and I were going to have a bite to eat, talk through a few things. Going to Dollops, you know, that little bistro round the corner. You care to join us?'

'That's very kind of you, Walter. I might. Yes, why not? Got to get out of my Wilkie Pole gear, so I should think I'd be along in about half an hour.'

'Fine. See you then.'

The producer and the comedian left. It was nine-thirty and the end of the studio session. The plugs were pulled out and everyone started to leave (straight to the bar). What hadn't been done would have to wait for the next, already over-crowded, day.

Charles stretched out for a few minutes, letting the tension drain from his limbs. The problem of an avenging Chox remained, but at least he had earned a brief reprieve. After five minutes, he felt almost human and started out for his dressing room.

It was when he got into the corridor that Charles saw Chox. The roadie was visible through the glass doors at the end. He looked jumpy and nervous, waiting.

A moment of panic stopped his mind dead. Then he started to think quickly. The corridor was a dead end, leading only to the Ladies' and Gents' lavatories. The only escape for him was back through the control room into the studio.

But even as he realised this, it was too late. In the shock of seeing Chox, he had moved back and was now nearer the lavatories than the control room. Just as he was about to step forward, the roadie turned suddenly towards him and pushed open the door into the corridor.

Instinctively, Charles leapt backwards and shoved his way into the Gents. As he did it, he saw his folly. He was trapped in a cul-de-sac.

He went to one of the cubicles and locked himself in. It would give him a little protection. If necessary, he supposed he could stay in there all night. And in the state he was in, the lavatory could be very useful.

He heard the click of the outer door as someone entered. Then silence. He waited for Chox to speak, or for a blow on the door, or for the appearance of that thin cruel face over the top of the cubicle.

There was nothing.

Then, again, the click of the outer door being opened.

This was followed sharply by the sound of another cubicle door being shut and locked. Presumably Chox had hidden himself from a potential witness.

The unseen newcomer seemed to take an unconscionably long time relieving himself, but eventually there was the swish of water in the wash-basin and the clank of the roller towel being pulled down. Followed by the soft thud of the outer door closing.

Once again Charles and Chox were the only people in the room. Playing a waiting game.

The silence was oppressive. Every hum of the air conditioning, every gurgle of the cisterns took on a new and menacing identity. But there was no human sound.

Time crawled by, broken-backed. Charles was sweating a lot. The more he thought about it, the less he liked the idea of waiting till someone else came in. Now the studio work had stopped, the building would be empty but for the security men and the crowd in the bar, many floors above. He looked at his watch. Quarter to eleven. The bar-flies would soon be making their meandering ways home to disgruntled wives, to disappointed second wives or with unsuitable PA's.

He couldn't face the idea of sitting there for another ten hours. Better confront whatever evil there was outside than let his imagination inflate it to terror proportions.

He swallowed deeply, then in one movement, slid back the bolt, opened the door and stepped outside.

No one.

The row of blue doors was uniform, all closed. He moved softly along, tense for attack, pushing against each door.

Each one gave inward to his pressure. Each cubicle was empty.

Until he came to the one nearest the entrance. That was locked on the inside.

Plucking up courage, he knocked on the door.

Nothing.

He called Chox's name.

There was no response.

He drew back and crouched to look under the door. He could see the end of a thin leg protruding from discoloured jeans. The foot was encased in a frayed grey plimsoll. He recognised Chox's clothes.

Still, fearing a trap, he found a lavatory brush and poked at the leg underneath the door. There was no movement.

He rang the security men from the studio control room. Two of them came. One climbed over the top of the cubicle and opened the door. He came out and the three of them looked inside.

Chox Morton was sitting on the closed lavatory seat, leaning back against the pipes. His eyes were closed and his sleeve rolled up to show the pitted terrain of his forearm. The other arm hung loose by his side and on the tiled floor, where it had dropped from his hand, lay a plastic syringe.

He was not breathing.

# Chapter XV

COMIC: I say, I say, I say, do you know why my girl-friend's called 'Television'?

FEED: No, I don't know why your girl-friend's called 'Television'.

COMIC: Because she never has much on on Saturday nights and she often does repeat performances on Sundays.

Charles had to spend a long time at the police station. There seemed to be no suspicion of foul play in Chox Morton's death, but the police were interested in what Charles had been doing hanging around the television premises in make-up and costume so long after the studio session had finished.

Since he didn't have enough evidence to start propounding his theory of Bill Peaky's murder, he had to make do with some rather incomplete excuses to justify his presence. He sweated for a bit while the police questioned him, but after a time they realised that, however suspicious his behaviour, he hadn't actually committed any crime. Having nothing to charge him with, they spoke to him sternly, took a statement about his discovery of Chox's body and let him go. They warned him that he might have to appear at the inquest and said they would be in touch to fix the details if necessary.

As, with some relief, he left the interview room,

Charles saw a middle-aged man in a discreet tweed suit sitting waiting on a chair in the corridor. He was about to walk past, but the man addressed him.

'Excuse me. I gather you are the one who found the body.'

'Yes.'

'Ah.' There was a pause. The man looked distressed, like the man from the ad with no life insurance at fifty-five. He seemed to want to talk, but have nothing to say. When he introduced himself, it was clear why he needed to communicate with someone. 'I'm Charles' father.'

'Charles?'

'I believe he had taken to calling himself Chox.'

'Oh. Yes. I'm sorry.'

It was a shock to see this conventional middle-class man and try to relate him to the dead roadie. Chox had seemed classless and rootless.

'I suppose I'm sorry too,' Mr Morton went on vaguely. 'More confused than anything at the moment. I mean, we'd hardly seen him for two or three years. When I saw the body, it could have been anyone. Oh, it is Charles all right, no question, but somehow he didn't seem to be anything to do with me. That's not the boy we put through prep school and Epsom College; it's another person. And to die of . . . that.'

'It must be terrible for you.'

'Yes, I suppose it is. I haven't been able to define my feelings yet. My mind still can't cope with the idea of Charles as a heroin addict. But I suppose when it can accommodate that, the idea of his dying of an overdose is a natural corollary.'

'The police are sure it was an overdose?'

'Oh, certainly.' Mr Morton looked at him in a bewildered way. 'Yes, apparently he had got hold of some particularly dangerous form of the drug. Well, they say it's not the drug in itself that's so dangerous in its pure form, but it's what it gets mixed with for sale by these . . . what are they called? Pushers?' He handled the jargon of drug culture with bemused unfamiliarity. He could not yet believe that any of the events of the last four hours had happened and was quoting verbatim from what he had just been told by the police. 'Apparently what he should have done, what the police recommend for addicts is that they should get registered with a doctor—it seems it happens a lot, there are standard procedures—and the doctor will prescribe what I think they call a maintenance dose and that sort of keeps the addict on the straight and narrow. Otherwise they are just at the mercy of these . . . pushers. Unfortunately it seems Charles was still trying to keep his addiction a secret, so he had to go to these . . . less reputable sources.'

The man was still talking very calmly, piecing together the unfamiliar, but Charles sensed that the tension was building up and soon Mr Morton was going to be swamped by a shattering wave of emotion. Selfishly, Charles didn't want to be around when that happened.

'Yes, it's a frightful business,' he said meaninglessly. 'I'm sorry, I must be off.'

'Yes.' Mr Morton did not appear to hear him. 'He was very young, you know.'

'How young?'

'Twenty-three. In January. He would have been. Twenty-three.'

A lot of factors prevented Charles from sleeping for what little of the night was left to him. First, there was the shock of what he had seen and the subsequent interviews at the police station. Next there was the half-tumblerful of Bell's he had drunk when he got back to Hereford Road; he found, unless alcohol put him straight to sleep, it had the opposite effect and condemned him to wakefulness. Also, somewhere in the back of his mind, there was nervous anticipation of the next day. In spite of the events of the night, *The New Barber and Pole Show* was still going to be recorded and it was potentially the most important event for some years in what Charles occasionally dignified with the title of his 'career'.

But more than all these deterrents to sleep, an ugly thought had been seeded and was growing in his mind, growing into a huge black plant that threatened to blot out all other thoughts.

Suppose Chox Morton's death had not been an accident . . .?

Charles could not forget the third person. When he had been locked in the lavatory and Chox had also been in the room, an unidentified third person had come in and Chox had hidden himself in another cubicle. The third person had, Charles remembered, taken an unconscionably long time to relieve himself.

If that was all he had been doing.

If, that is to say, he hadn't also been injecting Chox with dirty heroin.

Only one other person connected with the case knew that Chox was in the building.

The call was at ten for camera rehearsal. There would be a dress run at about four in the afternoon and the recording would start in front of the audience at seven forty-five.

Charles found Lennie Barber alone in his dressing room at a quarter to ten and decided that nothing was to be gained by prevarication.

'Lennie, Chox Morton died last night.'

'Good God. Did he?'

'Yes. I found him in a cubicle in the Gents. He died of a massive injection of adulterated heroin.'

'Silly little sod. I suppose it had to happen at some time. You can't go on living like that without it catching up on you.' The comedian spoke with not exactly pity, but world-weary acceptance.

'Lennie, I'm not convinced that Chox's death was an accident.'

Lennie Barber looked up at him sharply. Then smiled. 'Oh, Charles, here we go again. First it's Bill

Peaky, now it's Chox Morton. Can't you let anyone die a normal death? No doubt you'd regard cancer as evidence of foul play.'

But Charles wasn't going to be sidetracked. 'Lennie, I want to know what you did after you left me last night.'

The comedian's eyes narrowed. 'Oh, so that's it. That's the way your mind is going. Well, I'm not sure whether to be insulted or flattered.'

'I will be asking other people.' Charles tried ineffectively to cover his clumsiness.

'I see,' said Lennie Barber sardonically. 'Well, let me offer you my alibi. Straight after I left you I went, as I had said I would, with Walter Proud to this bistro place, Dollops, where, incidentally, they serve food which has reduced my guts to little knots of plastic hosepipe. However, that is not what you want to know. Walter and I arrived there at nine-fifteen, which is when he had booked the table for. The proprietor, called Gino, complimented us on our punctuality. From nine-fifteen until about twelve I was there eating and drinking, witnessed by about four waiters and assorted guzzlers and piss-artists. Want any more?'

'No, Lennie.' Charles left relief flooding through him. He had not enjoyed the ride on which his latest suspicions had been taking him. 'I'm sorry. I'm really sorry. But I had to ask.'

'Yes. You had to ask.'

'I'm sorry. I . . . Anyway, now I can enjoy the show.'

'All right for you. What about the poor audience?'

In the course of the morning Charles was summoned to the phone to take a call from the police. Yes, he would be required to appear at the inquest on Chox Morton in two days' time. No, it wasn't because anything had changed. It still seemed to be a straightforward case of self-inflicted drug overdose. Charles' presence was required because he was the person who had discovered the body.

Then the policeman said something which turned out

to be very comforting. 'Sorry you've got to turn up. I realise it's a nuisance. It's just bad luck that you were the one who found him. In fact, it could have been someone else.'

'What do you mean?'

'There was another bloke went into the lavatories just before you. While we reckon the body was there. Only he didn't look under the door. If he had he'd be the one we'd be dragging off to the inquest.'

'Who was he?'

'Oh, just a bloke who works for the company. Scene shifter, I think he is.'

And the third person was explained. Not a villain with murderous intent, just a scene shifter who needed a pee.

So there it was. Chox Morton had killed Bill Peaky. When he realised Charles was on to him, he had tried to kill his pursuer with the light-switch. Then he had tracked him down to the television studios and was out to get him. But he needed a fix. That would give him the confidence and steadiness he required for his next murder.

Unfortunately the latest batch of heroin he had bought was bad quality. Chox had passed out after the injection and never recovered consciousness.

It wasn't a solution that could ever be proved, but Charles knew it had to be right. Indeed, from the start of the case, it had looked unlikely that Charles would ever find proof of who had killed Bill Peaky; he had been relying on deducing the culprit and extracting some sort of confession. Chox was now past confession.

Charles had worked by educated guesswork and he reckoned he had got the answer right. But it was something he would have to keep for himself. He would not have the satisfaction of other people acknowledging his success.

He thought about the solution again, and again it worked. Not perfectly, but as near as made no difference.

Charles sometimes found himself thinking of life as a

series of circles, all of different sizes. No two quite fit on top of each other. Whether in a marriage or any other relationship, though the two personalities may seem to fit exactly, there is always a little overlap, a little sickle of discontent where the circles do not match.

And so it was with the case. Bill Peaky's death was the first circle and the conclusion that Chox Morton had killed him was the second. They didn't match exactly, without more information to fill out the second circle, but damned nearly. And nearly is about the best you can hope for in anything.

## Chapter XVI

COMIC: Did you hear about the television star who was so vain that every time he opened his fridge and the little light came on, he took a bow?

The audience for *The New Barber and Pole Show* was made up of coach-loads of people from social clubs. They were greeted by Charlie Hook, a little-known comedian who had been booked for the occasion as warm-up man. After five minutes of telling the audience they were all really wonderful people who were going to see a really wonderful show with some really wonderful artists and written by some really wonderful writers, he established that very few of those out front had ever seen a television recording before, so he started to explain a bit about the process. He explained that this company, unlike other companies, did not have signs which were held up saying 'Laugh' and 'Applaud', but if anyone missed any of the jokes, a big spike would come up through their seat. He explained that he should have welcomed the parties, which he proceeded to do, telling them all that they were really wonderful people and concluding by saying, 'And if there's a party of seventeen with red hair, I'll see her round in my dressing room afterwards.' With these and similar witticisms, he warmed the audience up. Or maybe softened them up. By the time he had finished they were all ready for a cosy evening's bingo. But not necessarily for *The New Barber and Pole Show.*

The audience wanted someone to make contact with them, to talk to them directly, but for the sake of the show, it should have been Lennie Barber and not Charlie Hook. Still, Charlie Hook had been booked and the theory was that his presence took the pressure off the star.

In Lennie Barber's case, it put the pressure on. For a start, here was competition from another comic. And, second, Charlie Hook was talking close to the audience, while Lennie was separated from them by thousands of pounds' worth of hardware, lumbering brutes of prehistoric proportions, the butting triceratops heads of cameras, the menacing pterodactyl spread of sound booms and the brontosauran bulk of cranes overhead. For a comedian who fed on audience response, it was death.

Charlie Hook introduced Barber to the audience with the assurance that he was a really wonderful person, and Lennie came forward to the warm-up mike to tell a few jokes and begin to make contact. But when he was half-way through his second gag, the Floor Manager indicated that it was time to start and the microphone went back to the really wonderful Charlie Hook who told the audience it was time to start.

From that point on, Lennie Barber had no opportunity to make up his lost contact with the audience. The logistics of recording the programme took over. There was a hell of a lot to fit in before nine-thirty when the plugs would be pulled out, and the comedian's schedule was a manic sequence of sketches and costume changes. With all the retakes made necessary by faulty camera work, fluffed lines or Wayland Ogilvie's dissatisfaction with the pictures *qua* pictures, there was no time for idle banter.

All the stops and starts broke the rhythm of Barber's performance. He needed, as he had done at the Leaky Bucket Club, to dictate his own pace, but here there were any number of factors, most of them mechanical, to prevent him from doing so. The strain was beginning to tell. In spite of the constant ministrations of dolly make-up girls, the comedian was sweating profusely and he looked his age. Suddenly to Charles it seemed cruel to put an old man through these savage hoops.

The more he felt the show going away from him, the harder Lennie Barber worked. His delivery grew louder, his takes bigger. Charles could see the sound boom operators wince as the comedian started to shout and no doubt in the box the size of the performance was causing the same reaction. It was getting too big for television, a medium that relies on subtle changes of intonation and eyebrow acting. Lennie Barber seemed to have forgotten about the camera; all he knew was that there was an audience out there that he had lost and he was doing his damnedest to win them back.

The climax came in his closing monologue. It was twenty past nine and no doubt relief was creeping into the control box because it looked likely that all the show would get recorded. But it had to go straight through to the end; there would be no time left for more retakes.

Perhaps knowing this, or perhaps just driven by a comedian's instinct for survival, Lennie Barber abandoned the script altogether. He advanced forward from the set, forcing the cameras to take ugly shots which included other cameras and equipment, and he addressed the audience directly. He was ill-lit and, from the television point of view, a disaster. But he was brilliant.

He went into a quick five minutes of his club act and, for the first time in the evening, he came alive. The jokes were mostly too blue ever to be televised and the weeks of rehearsal and agonising over the script all went for nothing.

But the audience roared. Suddenly here was something they could respond to. Not a neatly-packaged ersatz jokezak product viewed distantly and discontinuously from monitors, but a great comedian giving one of his greatest performances. It was five

minutes of brilliance, until the clock crept round to
nine-thirty and the anxious Floor Manager called a halt.

Charlie Hook's closing jokes went for nothing. The
audience had been spoiled by the sight of a real
comedian. The show too had presumably been spoiled.
In the box no doubt Wayland Ogilvie was calling down
curses on all Aquarians. But for Charles it had been one
of the most exciting moments of theatre he had ever
seen.

At the end of the recording he was standing behind
the set with one of the support actors who observed,
'Bloody unprofessional, wasn't it?'

'Bloody professional, I would have said. It was
brilliantly funny.'

'Yes, but it wasn't television, love, was it?'

Charles met Lennie Barber on the stairs going up to the
dressing rooms. The comedian looked old and
exhausted, but his face bore an expression of chastened
triumph, like a schoolboy who had just screwed his
headmistress. He knew he was going to be expelled, but
it had been worth it.

'End of my telly career, Charles,' he said
mischievously. 'Sorry about that. I hope you didn't
think this show was going to make your fame and for-
tune.'

'Not really.'

'Read a book once that said all comedians have got
this kind of death-wish thing. Well, that was my
kamikaze mission.'

'Had you planned it?'

'No. I just didn't want that audience to go home
cheated. They come here to be entertained and that was
the least they deserved. Come and have a drink.'

Inside his dressing room Lennie Barber opened
another bottle of Scotch. (He had got through one
already that day.) 'If I can't get rid of the pain in my
guts any other way, then I'll burn it out with alcohol.
Cheers.'

They drank gratefully. The recording, the camera rehearsal, the long, long day in the studio, might have taken place years before.

There was a knock on the door and Walter Proud came in. He wore his professional producer's smile and the firmness of his jaw showed the professional producer's determination never to admit disaster. 'Terrific, boys, really terrific. Lovely, Lennie. It's really going to be very big, this. Must go to a series and really turn the ratings on their heads.'

Lennie Barber didn't say anything. He just looked at the producer and smiled sceptically.

Walter Proud blushed. 'No, really. It'll edit together a treat,' he said defensively.

'Yeah, well, maybe.' Lennie Barber seemed to dismiss the possibility from his mind. 'Anyway, sorry I didn't use any of that extra material you got last night.'

'Oh, never mind. Didn't need it.'

'What extra material was that?' asked Charles curiously.

'Oh, Walter had got some one-liners from some other writers which he reckoned might help strengthen the monologues.'

'Yes, I only remembered it when we were in the restaurant last night,' said Walter, 'so I left Lennie eating away in Dollops and came back here to my office to get it.'

## Chapter XVII

FEED: Do you know, they say that whisky kills
    more people than bullets.
COMIC: Ah well, that's because bullets don't
    drink.

Charles got out of make-up as soon as he could and
hurried down to the bar. Everyone would be there, he
knew.

It was certainly crowded. Before diving into the
melée, he stood back and tried to see Walter through the
forest of bodies. No luck.

Near him Gerald Venables was talking to Nigel
Frisch. As he watched, the television executive moved
away and the solicitor caught his eye.

'Charles. Drink? Bell's, I take it.'

'Thanks. Have you seen Walter?'

'Over there somewhere. Hmm. I'm afraid not the
most stimulating evening I've ever spent.'

'No, not marvellous. Still, maybe it'll edit all right or
look better on the screen or something.'

'Maybe. Though, from what Nigel Frisch was saying,
we may never have the opportunity to find out.'

'You mean he's not even going to put it out?'

'Far be it for me to say that and then be proved
wrong. I'm sure anything he said to me was purely off
the record and I'm sure it'll be some time before the official verdict on the show filters down to you through

the official channels, but he gave me the impression that it might well not go out. In fact, to use his own words, he said he'd rather transmit an hour of rained-off cricket.'

'I see.' But Charles couldn't summon up much interest in the fate of *The New Barber and Pole Show*; his mind was seething with new thought about the deaths of Bill Peaky and Chox Morton.

'In fact,' Gerald continued, 'Nigel gave me the impression that they never had much faith in the project in the first place. But because they'd got a lot of staff and studios booked for the Bill Peaky Show, they thought they might as well do it on the off-chance.'

'I see. Yes, that sounds about right—get an old man to work his guts out for a fortnight on the off-chance—that's how television companies work.'

'There's no need to be satirical, Charles.'

'Look, are you going to get me that drink or not?'

'All right, all right. Keep your hair on. Is this deterioration in your customary sunny humour because of the show or because of the murder case? Incidentally, you must bring me up to date on that. Have you got a complete, perfect solution yet?'

'No, not yet.'

'Well, it's about time—'

'Give me half an hour.'

Walter Proud was standing at the bar guarding a large round of drinks. 'Ah, Charles, one of these is for you.' Charles reached out towards a Scotch. 'No, sorry, that one's Lennie's. Take this.'

Charles took the drink gratefully and took a long swallow for confidence. 'Walter, I wanted to—'

But the producer had turned away with outstretched arms. 'Lennie?'

The old comedian was sweating and looked ill, but he sat down on a bar stool and attacked the large whisky that was thrust into his hand.

'Well, Lennie, what did you think? Really?' Walter's

professional beam was fixed in place, He was trying to move them all from the knowledge that the show had been a disaster to the alcoholic reassurance that maybe it hadn't been so bad after all.

'I thought it was shit, if you want my honest opinion,' said Barber. 'Hardly worth editing, if you ask me.'

'Oh come on, it wasn't that bad.'

'Yes, it was, Walter. That bad, and far, far worse. So bad in fact that I don't want to talk about it. Let's talk about something else—talk about the telly shows we used to do back at Ally Pally. When it was live, when you just went on and did your act.'

'It wasn't so very different from now, Lennie.'

'Oh yes it was. We were different, for a start. We both had ambitions then, there were things we believed in. And we both enjoyed what we were doing. I was just flexing my muscles as a comic, beginning to be aware of what I could do. And you were locked away in your world of sound, fiddling with wires, screwdriver flashing away, touching up microphones. And not just microphones. The ladies. There are tales I could tell, Walter, about little dancers and—'

'Yes, I'm sure there are, Lennie, but I think you're being too pessimistic about what happened tonight. There were bits that—'

'There were bits that were awful and bits that were bloody awful. Why the whole . . . thing.' Lennie Barber suddenly slowed down. A strange expression flickered on to his face and stayed there. His words slurred. Not just the slurring of alcohol, the effect was too quick for that. 'What's . . . going on?' The words seemed unfamiliar, too large for his mouth, unmanageable. 'What . . . the hell's happened?'

He pushed away from the bar and made as if to step forward off his stool. But his legs would not support him and he collapsed on the bar-room floor.

## Chapter XVIII

COMIC: I say, I say, I say, do you know what is the most important skill for a stand-up comedian to have?

FEED: I don't know. What is the most important—

COMIC *(interrupting)*: Timing.

Charles and one of the barmen manhandled Barber up to his dressing room. As they were leaving the bar some loudmouth made a jokey remark about a few drinks too many and Charles had to restrain himself from punching the fellow's teeth in. Lennie Barber was suffering from something more than alcohol.

In the dressing room they laid him out on the divan and the barman went off to fetch the duty nurse. Charles looked down at the prostrate body with horror.

One side of Lennie Barber's stricken face smiled. 'You half cheer a bloke up, mate,' he managed to say. 'Do I really look that bad?'

'No, of course not.' Charles tried to smile too.

Lennie Barber breathed with difficulty. Spittle gathered and dripped unchecked from the corner of his mouth. He looked desperately ill.

Charles couldn't stand it. 'Lennie, do you think he put something in your drink?'

'My drink?' the slurred voice echoed. 'My drink? Who?'

'Walter.'

'Walter?' The frozen face twitched and a gurgling
sound issued from the sagging mouth. With sickened
understanding, Charles realised the comedian was
laughing. 'Oh, Charles . . . detective to the end. So keen
. . . and so . . . wrong.'

The door of the dressing room opened and the duty
nurse came in. She looked at Barber without betraying
any emotion, spoke to him and tested his reflexes. From
the left-hand side of his body there was no response. She
straightened up and said in a professional voice, 'I think
I'd better phone for an ambulance. Now don't worry.
I'm sure everything will be all right.' She turned to
Charles. 'Would you mind staying with him until I come
back?'

Wild tigers wouldn't have stopped him from staying
there. As soon as the door closed, he turned back to
Barber. 'What did you mean?'

'I mean you now . . . suspect Walter.' Each word was
dragged out and misshapen. 'They must keep making
new . . . sticks for you to grab . . . the wrong end of.'

'It wasn't Walter?'

Lennie tried to shake his head, but the muscles would
not obey him. 'I . . . I killed Bill Peaky.'

'You? And Chox Morton?'

'Yes.'

'But how? I don't understand.'

'No you . . . don't. Never did understand. You know
how . . . Bill Peaky died. I worked it out . . . planned
. . . pulled out the cable with the . . . cart on purpose.'

'And then changed the wires in the interval? But
how could you—with your burnt hands? You couldn't
handle a screwdriver.'

'No, Charles. Credit me with some . . . subtlety.
What kind of . . . murderer fiddles around with a . . .
screwdriver? I had a wrongly wired extension lead made
up and . . . switched the two round.'

'Oh.' For a moment Charles felt very stupid. 'But
why did you kill Chox? And how did you kill him, come

to that? You were in the restaurant when he was in-
jected.'

'Oh, Charles, Charles. Use your . . . intelligence.
With a heroin addict you don't have to be there. Just
. . . give him the . . . tools and he will . . . finish the job.'
This parody of Winston Churchill prompted another
spasm of rasping laughter. 'All I had to do was give . . .
Chox the dirty heroin and let him . . . kill himself in his
own . . . time.'

'But how did you come to be giving him heroin?'

'Come on, you've missed so . . . much. You may not
be bad at impersonating Wilkie . . . Pole, but as a detective . . . you're rubbish. Chox was . . . blackmailing
me.'

'How was I meant to know that?'

'You were there when he started it . . . if you could
put two and . . . two together.'

'When?'

'At that club in Sutton. When his band broke up. He
knew then he was out of a . . . job. No money. So he . . .
challenged me.' Lennie Barber stopped, gasping. The
strain of speech on his unresponsive body was enormous.

'You mean when he started talking about Bill Peaky's
death and the terrible things he had seen that day, he
was telling you he had witnessed what you had done?'

Lennie acknowledged this with an exhausted wave of
his right hand.

'But how had he seen you?'

'Lighting . . .' the comedian murmured.

'From the lighting store. He was in the lighting
store?' Again a tiny wave. 'What, he had locked himself
in there to give himself a fix, because the lock on the
lavatory door was broken, and while he was in there, he
saw you switching the extension leads?'

This time Lennie Barber managed a soft 'Yes.'

'But why didn't he tell the police at the time?'

'H . . . heroin.'

'He didn't want them to find out he was an addict?'

'Yes.'

'And he would have kept quiet about it forever, but then he lost his job and saw you as a potential source of money. Which is why you had to borrow from me in the bar, although you'd told me you never borrowed money. Oh, my God, I've been stupid.' Now the one great boulder had been moved by confession, other smaller stones of fact were dislodged and started tumbling down in the avalanche of logic. 'So, when I started suspecting Chox and told you, you had to try and keep us apart. You set up the switch in his room—I remember now, when I arrived you came out of the house with some specious story. You'd broken in . . . how?'

'Credit card . . . in the lock.'

'And you hoped to frighten me off, but you weren't sure that you had, so when Chox came to the studios . . . But why did he come if he wasn't after me?'

'Money,' Barber mouthed painfully.

'Oh, I see. He'd come for his next instalment. But, rather than give him the money to buy the heroin, you gave him the heroin itself. Adulterated heroin. And so he died.'

Again the frozen features managed a smile as Barber pronounced, 'Got . . . there . . . at last.'

'OK, Lennie, I see how you did it, but I still don't understand why. No, I take that back. I understand why you killed Chox. You had to, if you weren't to pay him off for the rest of your life and always go in fear of discovery. But why did you kill Bill Peaky?'

There was a pause. When the voice came, it was very weak. 'He . . . didn't matter.'

'What do you mean?'

'He was . . . nothing.'

'Yes, from what I've heard of him, I agree, but you don't kill someone for that. Why did you kill him?'

There was a long silence. 'He . . . passed a remark about my . . . father.'

The words sounded so feeble, the reason for murder so pathetic, and yet Charles could feel through them the

enormous ground-swell of resentment that they
represented. The clash of two traditions, on the one
side, the long history of music hall, of hard work and
foul digs for insufficient money, of talent flourishing
unrecognised in provincial flea-pits; and on the other,
the smart world of television, instant stardom,
mushroom reputations fed with all the conveniences and
luxuries of script-writers, sycophantic production teams
and sharp agents. Given that background, he could understand how a single remark from the swaggering
young comedian about the old comedian's idolised
father could have signed his death-warrant. Lennie
Barber was beyond morality; for him Bill Peaky was
nothing but an ugly parasite on the surface of the earth
and, as such, to be removed.

The long talk had taken its toll on the comedian. His
breathing was slower and the moving eye in his twisted
face was heavy. Charles sat with him quietly, wondering
whether he had lost consciousness.

But no. The eye flickered again and the voice, soft
and distorted almost beyond recognition, murmured.
'Funny, you know I needed . . . Wilkie Pole . . . the
bastard.'

Once more he seemed to pass out, but after a long
moment he spoke again. This time the voice was clearer,
stronger. 'Funny . . . a stroke . . . Never thought of a
stroke . . . Thought it would be the old guts.'

The idea seemed to give him satisfaction. Maybe it
was the knowledge that he had finally escaped his
father's shadow, that he was not destined to die of a
perforated ulcer backstage at the Derby Hippodrome.

He didn't speak again after that and was unconscious
when the ambulance men arrived.

Charles wandered back down to the bar in a daze. It had
only just closed. His interview with Barber had taken no
more than twenty minutes. He met Gerald Venables
pulling on his immaculate camel overcoat.

'Well, Charles,' said the solicitor urgently. 'You said

you'd know who killed Bill Peaky in half an hour and that was half an hour ago. Do you know who did it?'

'Yes.'

'Who?'

'Chox Morton,' said Charles Paris.